THE HOUSE OF DEAD MAIDS

Books by Clare B. Dunkle

THE HOLLOW KINGDOM TRILOGY:

The Hollow Kingdom
BOOK I

Close Kin
BOOK II

In the Coils of the Snake
BOOK III

———◆———

By These Ten Bones

THE HOUSE OF DEAD MAIDS

CLARE B. DUNKLE

illustrations by PATRICK ARRASMITH

SQUARE
FISH

HENRY HOLT AND COMPANY
NEW YORK

SQUARE FISH

An Imprint of Macmillan

Library of Congress Cataloging-in-Publication Data
Dunkle, Clare B.
The house of dead maids / Clare B. Dunkle ;
[illustrations by Patrick Arrasmith].
p.   cm.
Summary: Eleven-year-old Tabby Aykroyd, who would later
serve as housekeeper for thirty years to the Brontë sisters, is taken from
an orphanage to a ghost-filled house, where she and a wild young boy
are needed for a pagan ritual.
ISBN 978-0-312-55155-1
[1. Household employees—Fiction.   2. Ghosts—Fiction.   3. Rites and
ceremonies—Fiction.   4. Orphans—Fiction.   5. Brontë family—
Fiction.   6. Great Britain—History—19th century—Fiction.]
I. Arrasmith, Patrick, ill.   II. Title.
PZ7.D92115Hou 2010   [Fic]—dc22   2009050769

Originally published in the United States by Henry Holt and Company
First Square Fish Edition: September 2011
Square Fish logo designed by Filomena Tuosto
Book designed by April Ward
macteenbooks.com

10 9 8 7 6 5 4 3 2 1

AR: 6.0 / LEXILE: 930L

Sometimes, when the ghosts
and goblins swarm,
all a child can count on
is the help of another child.

I love you, Jennifer.
You've always been there.

CHAPTER ONE

I WAS NOT the first girl she saw, nor the second, and as to why she chose me, I know that now: it was because she did not like me. She sat like a magistrate on the horsehair sofa, examining me for failings. "Stop staring," she snapped. "You'd think I was a world's wonder."

I looked away, thinking my own thoughts. She couldn't stop me from doing that. She had a sweep of thick brown hair tucked up into a bun, and she wore a somber black wool dress. Her hands were soft: lady's hands. Her face was anything but soft.

It looked cold and hard and pale, like stone. Like a newly placed tombstone.

"I mustn't take a half-wit, though," she said reluctantly, as if she would like to do it. She seemed to consider idiocy the greatest point in my favor.

"Oh, our Tabby's no half-wit," countered Ma Hutton. "She just has that look. You did say you wanted to see an ugly one, miss."

I stared at the braided rag rug, thinking about the black dress. She was in mourning. For whom? She was a handsome woman and might once have been beautiful.

"Tabby's the best knitter in the school," Ma Hutton was proclaiming. "She can turn out a sock in a day. And handy! She's stronger than she looks, and she sews a pretty buttonhole, miss."

"No scars," interrupted the woman. "You can swear to that, you said. This is of the utmost importance. I cannot bear deformity."

"She hasn't a scar that I recollect," Ma Hutton said slowly, beginning to fidget with her hands. She was wanting to knit, I knew. She hated to put down her knitting. "Tabby hasn't worked in the fields, have you, child? She's done light work."

"No broken bones? I must be positive on this point."

Ma Hutton signed for me to speak.

"I've broken naught, miss," I answered, meeting the woman's gaze as a token I was telling the truth. She winced, and her eyes glittered. When a dog looked like that, people knew to leave it alone.

"No relations, you said," she reminded Ma Hutton, turning away from me.

"None, miss," Ma Hutton assured her. "Tabby doesn't even know where she's from."

Before a kindly soul had brought me to Ma Hutton's knitting school, I had grown up in the kitchens of big houses, polishing boots and running errands. I had been told that my surname was Aykroyd, although I knew no one else who had it. Most likely it had been my mother's name. I could dimly recall a face when I thought of *mother*, although the face was so young and frightened that it confused me. The one thing I held as a certainty had been dinned into my ears by angry cooks and housekeepers. I had no father at all, quite a failing in a little child.

"She'll do," said the woman. "Tell her to fetch her things."

I hadn't much to take from the room I shared with eight other girls, except an old greatcoat someone had given me out of charity and the pattens, or wooden clogs, which we wore outside in the mud.

Then I went to the room where Ma's students sat knitting and bade them good-bye.

One of the girls who had been passed over came to whisper with me in the doorway. "She's been here before, that woman," she said. "She took Izzy with her last time."

I said, "I don't remember a girl named Izzy."

"It was years ago, when I was new here. Izzy must be grown now, and run away with a soldier most likely, and miss needs a new girl to beat with her hairbrush. I got a shivery feeling when she talked to me. Didn't you? I wouldn't be you for a thousand pounds."

I returned to the parlor. Money had changed hands while I was gone, a substantial sum by the look of things because Ma Hutton's typical good humor had blossomed into rapture. She went so far as to wax sentimental over me, though I had never been a favorite, and bade me keep my knitting needles and my ball of worsted in its little rag pocket as a parting gift from the school. "And wrap up warm," she counseled, pulling the greatcoat around me. "I don't doubt you'll have a long journey." But where we were going, I hadn't the heart to ask, and no one bothered to say.

We were in April then, but the spring had been

cold, and the day was misty, as dark at noon as it had been at dawn. The houses across the street looked gray and insubstantial, shadows rather than stone.

The woman in black pushed me towards an open cart waiting in the lane. Its driver had taken the precaution of bringing a lighted lantern with him, and he swung down from the seat and held up the light to view me. "What have you brought us?" he boomed. "Why, it's a quaint little body, to be sure!"

It isn't that I'm so bad to look at, for my nose is straight and I have all my teeth, but my eyelashes are sparse and pale, and my eyes are no particular color. Add to that my stature, which is very small, and you'll find folks who call me a quaint body yet.

The man who bent over me was long-limbed, with a round face buffeted red by wind and weather. "Pleased to meet you, little maidie," he said, shaking hands. "My name's Arnby. You look a right canny lass. How old would you happen to be?"

"I'm eleven, sir. My name's Tabitha Aykroyd, but people call me Tabby."

"So many years packed in such a tiny frame! I can tell she's got us a good one. Now, listen, little maid. If she gives you any cause for grief," and he nodded towards the woman who stood behind me, "just you come tell me all about it, and I'll soon set her to rights."

This alarmed me, as it seemed an impertinence. I didn't want to start off badly with my new employer. "Please, miss," I said, turning to the woman, "what am I to call you?"

She made no reply, but pushed past me and scrambled awkwardly onto the seat of the cart. Arnby stood by and laughed to see her do it.

"She'd tell you to call her Miss Winter if she could swallow her pride to speak," he said. "But call her the old maid, dearie. Everyone else does."

Our journey took two long, tedious, dreadfully foggy days. The creeping mist swallowed us up and showed neither landmark nor horizon, and often Arnby had to walk ahead and lead the horse by the bridle. It seemed to me that we jolted up and down and went nowhere at all. I tried to knit my sock, but the cart shook so that it made me ill.

"It's wondrous weather," declared Arnby once, climbing back onto his seat. "The season's so late that the ewes have lost lambs, and the planting's only half done. The old earth's tired, that's what, and last year's storms and floods have vexed her. People don't think on the earth enough, and that's what causes the trouble. They plow at her and rip food from her, toss their trash and middens on her, bore mine holes into her, and never a word of thanks do they say."

"Shut up, old fool," snapped Miss Winter.

They were like that the whole journey, silent or quarrelling, and I was sorely puzzled how to take it. At first, I had cast Miss Winter in the role of housekeeper and Arnby as a servant, but seeing him speak so free, I thought he must be the farm steward and she a maid or cook. Soon I didn't know what to think, nor what their relation might be. I couldn't imagine steward and housekeeper taking such a frightful journey together, and that just to fetch home a new maid.

The matter must have weighed on my mind, for as I dozed, I dreamt a strange thing. "Just you try it," I thought I heard Arnby say, and his voice was as soft as silk. "I'll grab you before you take two steps and smash your skull like pie crust. Why else do you think I brought my staff? We don't need you, you know. Not the maids."

I sat up in a great fright at this, sure I'd fallen in with robbers, but the two of them were silent, sitting side by side on the cart bench the same as they always did.

Arnby heard me move and smiled over his shoulder. "The little maidie's been winking," he said. "Did you have good dreams? Take care you don't catch cold." And he reached back to tuck me up warm in some sacking.

Partway through the second day, we left the horse and cart at a farmhouse and proceeded in a little open boat. Arnby plied the oars vigorously to make progress upriver. I found that mode of travel more interesting at first, for the fog couldn't hold to the surface of the water where the current flowed, but tore into streamers or hung above us like a flimsy ceiling. When I looked to the shore, I could make out a few feet of steep bank here and there, or a line of trailing underbrush. Now and then I caught a glimpse of cliff walls.

But it was very gloomy on the river, with cold drops sliding down our hair and wetting our clothes; I soon was damp through and wished the endless bumping about would end. Then the river narrowed to a stream, shallow but fast, and Arnby had hard work to pole along the bottom. The night drew in, and Miss Winter began to fuss and scold, and I curled up in my greatcoat and tried to sleep to get away from them both.

How it ended I barely knew, but I remember

the light shining on a small beach of shingle and Arnby carrying me along, while Miss Winter held the lantern before us and looked like nothing but a white face and a pair of hands with her black dress swallowed up in the night. I didn't want to be held and would have liked to get down, but protesting the point seemed so like their bickering that I did not know how to do it politely, and at the last I felt so tired and unhappy that I did not do it at all.

And that is how I came to my new house, carried in like a wax doll, and a bad business it was then, and a worse business to follow.

CHAPTER TWO

I WOKE FROM a heavy sleep to the sound of a person shaking down the ashes at the hearth, but when I opened my eyes, I saw only the dense shade of a little cloth room. A moment later, a woman pushed back heavy green folds beside me, and light streamed in and lit up twinkling motes of dust. I was in a curtained bed so large that I could stretch out both arms and not reach its sides, and so high that I had to climb down a wooden stepladder drawn up beside it. I might have hurt myself tumbling over the edge.

"Whose room is this?" I ventured to inquire, awed at my surroundings.

"Chamber for the young maid," muttered my companion. "Come to the hearth. You've got to be measured."

She took a string from around her neck and held it at my collarbone while she bent to check its length to the floor, marking the intervals on it with a chunk of coal. She had a broad, dumpy figure and freckled arms with dimples at the wrists, sparse grizzled hair, gray eyes that studied the world with sour disinterest, and a seamed mouth cinched up tightly like a miser's purse.

"Where is the other girl?" I asked, turning around so she could find the span of my shoulders.

"We got no other girls," she said. "Just the old maid and you."

The morning light shone through a small window set with uneven diamond panes of blue and amber glass, throwing a harlequin pattern onto the wooden floor and brown gritstone walls. In the corner towered a great oak clothes press decorated with puffing faces and roaring animal heads. By the bed, a little table held an earthenware pitcher and washbowl, and next to me at the hearth stood an upright chair, with my garments laid across it to dry. A very old mirror hung by the door. Fashioned into its bead-work frame were fanciful scenes of fighting birds, but the glass was so smoky and streaked that it returned little by way of a reflection.

"I heard the other girl in my sleep," I said. "I heard her get up and wash. See, the other pillow's dented." And I pointed at the bed.

The woman didn't stop to look. She worked her pursed mouth into a frown until she looked like a pug dog. "We got no other girls," she said stubbornly. "Just a few silly village lasses, and they won't come in at this season."

She lapsed into silence, and I held up my arms so that she could measure my waist. When she was fin-ished, she checked her marks, grunted, and straight-ened up. "Name's Mrs. Sexton," she told me. "I keep the house. Maybe tonight, maybe tomorrow, the master's coming back with a child for you to look after. Till they arrive, you can do as you like." She wrapped the measuring string around her neck and turned to quit the chamber.

"A child!" I said, surprised. "A little one? I'm to be nursemaid?"

"I don't know his age," she muttered. "When you want food, come to the kitchen." And with that, she was gone.

After washing and dressing, I ventured out to find the kitchen, a harder task than it would seem. I went down the dark passage outside the bed-chamber and found a little back staircase, but it led into a part of the house that wasn't used. I wandered there for some time from room to room, trying locked doors.

If I liked, I could look ahead in my tale and declare that the house felt sinister, but all I knew at the time was that I didn't like it. It was large and labyrinthine, and, owing to its harsh setting, very poorly lit. The wind was its most active visitor, prowling about ceaselessly, rattling the casements and sobbing in the chimneys; thus, the stone walls were strong and thick, and the windows small and few. Fortunate was that chamber which held a double casement of clear lights. Most held, as mine did, a few small panes of amber glass. The corridors might as well have been passages in a crypt, for they had no windows at all.

I could believe that the house had no maids, as dirty as the chambers were. A froth of dust covered their surfaces. The furniture was muffled in canvas sheets, looking more like some pale shrubbery sprouting in the corner than a chair or table fashioned for the use of men. Many rooms were bare of ornament save a few grotesque old paintings and the omnipresent covering of grime.

In the end, I rediscovered my narrow stair and went back up, took another turning, came upon a second little stair, and found the kitchen at last. A clean place it was, too, I was happy to see, with a big bare wooden table and a great roaring fire. Mrs. Sexton was settled before the glowing hearth on a bench, her mending basket beside her and a clay pipe clamped between her teeth. Not another creature was there to enjoy the glorious warmth except the poor plucked fowls who lay next to the stew pot.

She served me oatcakes and butter in silence, but her portions were generous, and my feelings towards her mellowed.

"Where is Miss Winter?" I asked as I ate.

"You mean the old maid, don't you," she muttered. "She's in bed. No telling if Her Majesty means to get up this fine day."

The kitchen was blessed with two large windows through which I could see a bit of vegetable garden, a rock wall, and some ragged bushes bowing low before the wind. Behind these rose a steep green slope, with shadow and sun sweeping across it as unseen clouds hurried by.

"Shall I take her a tray then?" I asked as I rose from the table.

"If the old maid wants food, she can come here for it, same as you," said Mrs. Sexton. "She's naught to you, and she's not your friend. Don't be doing her favors." And she turned away from my questions, leaving me more confused than before.

I found myself at liberty once my breakfast was done. Mrs. Sexton steadfastly refused to set me a task. At one of my old houses, the master's return would have meant a troop of twenty maids chattering and laughing and cleaning everything from top to bottom. Here I was the only maid, and yet it seemed I was no maid at all, only a nurse for visiting children. Not for as long as I could recall had I been without employment of some kind, and the prospect of a day of idleness rather daunted me. Not wishing Mrs. Sexton to think me stupid, however, I resolved to return to the bedchamber assigned to me and puzzle out what to do.

Back I went into the dim passageways, a tangle of turnings as twisted as a lover's knot. With my belly full and no employment to hurry me along, I rambled at my leisure. Room let onto room in inconvenient arrangements, and steps ran up or down in the most inexplicable fashion. Some chambers exhibited great extravagance in the form of elaborate stained glass or magnificently painted ceilings, but the entire place seemed to belong to a bygone age.

Here is the answer, I thought: the master has better houses and comes here but seldom. Probably he's close with his money and resists paying wages to maintain such a monstrous old castle. He'll stay locked in with his agents while he's here, turn a blind eye to the dust, and leave as soon as he can. And what will I do then? For surely he'll take his child with him.

Dismayed by these musings, I found myself liking the place less and less. There was little of cheer or comfort about it. Such decoration as I came upon breathed a predatory spirit, dominated by the steel relics of war. Pikes and halberds, chain mail, and crossed arrows adorned the walls. Upon one heavy sideboard clustered a trio of cannonballs in little hollows, and on a chest of drawers sat a cavalier's helmet. Everywhere were hunting trophies in the form of animal skins, or antlers, the weapons of the beast.

To fix my bearings, I looked out the windows whenever the glass would permit a view. To the west, the great green ridge rose up behind the house and loomed over us like a frozen wave, but it gave no shelter, for the house stood on a mound or hill far enough out from it to catch the winds that came tumbling down its slope. To the east, and well below us, I caught glimpses of the silver curves of the stream that had brought me there, and close by its bank, the dark roofs of a small village. North lay stark moorland, rising into blunt, rocky crests and falling into treeless valleys, a desolate place devoid of shelter or human habitation, the haunt of the fox, the plover, and the solitary crow.

No window looked south.

I found when I returned to my bedchamber that someone had been in to tidy it, and the green curtains around the bed were tied back. This hardly seemed like the work of Her Majesty, Miss Winter. Mrs. Sexton must have come in to take care of it, but she had left the work half done. The door to the bottom cabinet of the clothes press was standing open. Next to it on the floor ranged a neat line of small objects. I came close and found that they were feathers.

A board that formed the bottom of the clothes press had been tilted up to reveal a shallow compartment between it and the floor. Within that compartment were a great many objects of charm but little value. One by one, I took the items out and arranged them next to the feathers. There were any number of curious buttons, as well as two striped snail shells and the tiniest bird's egg I could imagine, five foreign coins, a cracked game piece fashioned like a horse's head, and a pebble as round as the moon. Beneath them lay several slips of paper and two small worked samplers. The ink on the pages had faded and the paper darkened until the pen strokes were all but indistinguishable, and the samplers were stiff and brittle with age.

Then I had a surprise. At the back of the compartment lay a sock, an old friend in a crowd of strangers, for it was the style we knitted at Ma Hutton's school. I pictured the girl Izzy, who had come to this house before me, chancing upon this delightful little hoard. I looked at the neat line of feathers. Then I put the objects back into their hiding place, jumped to my feet, and ran downstairs.

I found Mrs. Sexton in the kitchen, chopping carrots for the stew. "A person has been in that room," I told her.

She gave me a sidelong glance. "What room?" she asked, and this silenced me for a few troubled moments. On no account could I bring myself to call it mine.

"That room you put me in," I declared at last.

"Somebody has been in it. Somebody has been playing!"

I expected her to deny it, and I was prepared with my facts. I knew that none but a child would treasure that little hoard, or treat those feathers with such care. But Mrs. Sexton merely cinched her wrinkled lips tighter around the stem of her pipe.

A clatter of pattens in the hallway just then brought me out of the kitchen at a trot, but by the time I reached the door, the person had gone. I heard the clatter go by again just out of sight around a corner, but another empty corridor was my reward. At length, I followed the sound to a bright, clean passage. I tried a door and found a pleasant parlor there, and Miss Winter glanced up from her book.

"Have you brought tea?" she inquired. A clock on the mantel chimed five, the only clock I had seen in the whole house.

"I was looking for the girl," I confessed. "I thought she came in here. Mrs. Sexton said there isn't a girl, but there is. She's been in the room where I sleep."

"She comes and goes," said Miss Winter. "I'm sure she'll find you when she wants to. Tell that worthless woman in the kitchen I want my tea."

I stood in the doorway for a bit, but she didn't look up or speak again, and I was too cowed to ask questions. Perhaps the other girl is simple, I thought, returning to the kitchen. Perhaps she's not as she should be, and that makes the servants loath to mention her to strangers. It isn't worth a quarrel, after all. And I persuaded Mrs. Sexton to let me take Miss Winter her tea, just for the pleasure of having an occupation.

We ate our own meal in the kitchen, sharing the big wooden table between us. I loitered by the fire until the heat made me sleepy, and when Mrs. Sexton saw me nodding, she took me up to bed. She tended the fire, passed a pan of hot coals between the sheets to warm them and turned the key in the lock as she left.

Late at night, the other girl returned to our chamber and climbed into bed with me. And, oh, how cold she was! The arms that twined around me were icy, and her dress was wringing wet. I grew cold to my bones as I hugged the thin form, attempting to warm it up. Vague fears troubled me, and Miss Winter's stern figure haunted my sleep: nothing but a white face and hands, with her dress swallowed up in the night.

When morning came, my little companion was gone, but not my indignation, and I was quite short with Mrs. Sexton when she pushed back the curtains on the bed.

"The other girl was here last night," I said severely, "and you needn't pretend she wasn't. What a state she was in! She'll catch her death, the way you let her run about in wet things."

Mrs. Sexton only stared at me. Then she heaved a sigh and turned to tend to the fire.

"You needn't lock the door anymore, either," I added. "It didn't keep her out."

"Lock's not for them," muttered Mrs. Sexton. "Lock's for you, to keep you from wandering the house at night and waking me up."

"I can be trusted to stay where I'm put," I answered as I climbed down the wooden stepladder. "What's that?"

A handsome dress lay on the chair over my old one. The cloth of it was sturdy and new, and if it lacked the layers of petticoats that were the fashion in town, this did nothing to diminish my growing joy, for as I held the dress up, I could see beyond all doubt that it had been made for no one but me.

"The village finished it last night," said Mrs. Sexton, ignoring my pleasure to scrape the ashes.

I smoothed the wide skirts, my bad temper

forgotten at the amazing news that a village had worked together to clothe me. The dress was black, as black and perfect as a crow's wing, a miniature copy of Miss Winter's imposing garment. "I can wear this to church today," I said, and that put the capstone on my delight. Never had I so much as dared to dream of poor ugly little Tabby Aykroyd showing off a new dress in church.

"Church?" asked Mrs. Sexton, pausing to eye me askance.

"It's the Lord's Day," I reminded her. "Oh, dear! I need to wash. What time do the house staff leave for service?"

"Wash if you like and go where you like," said Mrs. Sexton. "I stay here." And she picked up her bucket and left the room.

This put me in a predicament. Weekly service was inevitable, inescapable, as firmly fixed in the cycle of existence as the baking of the household loaves of bread. Now I asked myself, did I want to go to church? And the answer was by no means simple. Sometimes a curate had the gift of preaching, but more often than not, service was a contest of endurance to see whether the preacher's voice would give out before I lost the feeling in my dangling toes.

The thought that I might choose—that I might go or not as I pleased—awakened in me guilty relief.

I did have a suspicion that the quarrelsome, untruthful behavior of the residents of this house could not be improved by their impiety and that I should seek a different course if I did not wish to become like them. Nonetheless, such is the frailty of human goodness that I soon stifled this counsel with a dozen practical suggestions. Before I had concluded washing, I had decided to remain at home. Already I viewed my absence from divine worship that day with melancholy regret, as though it were a circumstance that had happened long ago instead of an event that had yet to take place.

I blush to own that this regret was quite drowned out by another, and that was the lack of an adequate looking glass. The old one in the beaded frame returned only a suggestion of features. I longed to see my new clothes, and as I stepped into the passage, I was just turning over in my mind where I might have seen a better mirror. When first I caught sight of the small figure in black, I thought it was my reflection.

She stood very still in the dusky passage where the light was poorest. Like me, she wore the black dress that proclaimed her a maid of the house, but where mine was new, hers was spoiled by mildew and smears of clay. Thin hair, dripping with muddy water, fell to her shoulders in limp, stringy ropes. This was my companion of the night before—and she was dead.

The dead hold no terrors for me. I have watched by the beds of those who have passed on, comforted by their sorrowless repose. But this little maid was a ghastly thing, all the more horrible because she stood before me. It wasn't the pallid hue of her grimy face that shocked me, or her little gray hands and feet. It was the holes where her eyes should have been, great round sockets of shadow.

The dead girl opened her lips as if she meant to speak. Her mouth was another black pit like the black pits of her eyes. She was nothing but a hollowed-out skin plumped up with shadow. I had the horrible idea that if I were to scratch her, she would split open, and the darkness within her would come pouring out.

I remember that she reached out a hand towards me, and I remember running away. I remember throwing open the door to the kitchen, and Mrs. Sexton's startled curse. I stood for long minutes by the bright, sunlit window, my teeth chattering uncontrollably. The comprehension that this was the icy form I had held through the night sputtered across my nerves and set the room to spinning.

Then Mrs. Sexton brought a glass, and brandy coursed through me like fire. Sense returned, and with it, an overpowering fervor. This had been a judgment upon me. I needed no other sign.

"I'm going to church!" I gasped.

CHAPTER THREE

MRS. SEXTON didn't hinder me with questions, which would have made me worse again. Seeing that I couldn't eat, she tied up bread and cheese in a napkin and sent it along with me. Not five minutes later, I stood trembling in the sunshine of a breezy spring day, as glad of my escape from that dark house as I had been of anything in my life.

The kitchen garden shone with dew, and the green slope of the great ridge climbed into the sky before me, facing the rising sun. I pushed past a sheep gate in a low stone wall and came around the side of the house. Then I discovered why I had seen no southern windows the day before. This side of the house was a long high barn with stables. Nor had the barn seen kinder treatment than the house: weeds grew in pens where the farrowing sow should lie, and the stalls stood empty, their paint peeled and faded. Only a few black-and-white hens scratched here and there in the barnyard and squawked their displeasure as the gusts caught them crosswise and sent them round like weathervanes.

Letting myself out the barnyard gate, I came to the front of the house, with a broad door in the middle of it and fancy lettering carved overhead. The village was out of sight beneath the brow of the hill, but I chose a likely path, scooped into a deep brown rut by generations of feet and littered with loose rocks. As I picked my way along it, drinking in the clean air, the gray phantom I had left behind began to lose its horror.

When I was nine, I had helped to nurse our curate's family during a fever. We lost them over several months, first the wife and babies and finally the curate himself, but not before that gentle man had made a lasting impression upon me. He liked to talk of godly things as he lay on his sickbed, and he gladly answered any question my childish mind could pose. He had not doubted that his family waited for him in the joyous kingdom of the Lamb, and when once I had asked him about *ghosts*, he had swiftly assured me that the dead do no harm to the living. My desire to attend worship this morning had much to do with that good man, whose conviction upon this point I longed to share, though I was in no wise convinced.

But when I entered the village on the bank below, I found no stone church, nor parsonage, nor parson, but only a little plot of graves on the green, with headstones plain and square. The village matrons were taking advantage of the sunny weather to wash their laundry and had produced in adjacent dooryards a great boiling of kettles. The brazen spectacle of work thus commenced on the Sabbath fairly took away my breath.

The children spotted me first and ran to their mothers, who left their work to watch my progress. They appeared cloddish, though I say it, who am no beauty myself; the common run were short and wide, like Mrs. Sexton, with thick limbs and sloping backs. They did not greet me, but stared, and I heard a murmur of "young maid" repeated from mouth to mouth. That woke in me the memory of what I owed these dull people; and when one of them approached me, I endeavored to thank her for my new dress. She did not reply, but she took out her thimble and touched it to me, with the air of one performing a rite.

I turned away much astonished and continued my quest, and they followed me, pointing and murmuring; but my path soon found the bank of the shallow brook and lost itself in river gravel, where several boats lay pulled up at the edge of the water, and Arnby's among them. I had no desire to wet my feet, so I walked back through the village accompanied by the whispering throng. I was not sorry when they halted at the little graveyard and we parted ways.

Going up the path was harder than coming down, and not only because of the climb. I had found no help for my troubles. My heart was heavy and my nerves were at a stretch; and then, there was the discouraging spectacle of the big brown house above me, brooding upon the brow of its hill, and the great green ridge rising above it and brooding over all.

Not anxious to return so soon to the haunted place, I turned aside to follow a faint trail that took me out of sight of both house and village. It ended at a doorway of arched stones set into the hillside, and a thick studded door standing open. Within I spied a straight passage, walled and flagged with wet stones, that angled up as it bored through the hill. It came to me that this must be another way into the house, or at least into its cellars, a shortcut to save the backs of tradesmen bringing supplies up from boats. I even thought I could see gray light falling into it from the other end some distance off.

I took a few steps along it, but the gloom oppressed me, and the odor of damp earth brought back the memory of what I had seen as strongly as if the little gray corpse stood in the passage beside me. Before I knew what I was about, I had turned and run back to the friendly daylight. There I stood for a few seconds, gasping.

Boots scraped the flagstones behind me, and Arnby came striding out of the passage, with dirt clinging to his trousers and a spade over his shoulder. "It's the little maidie!" he cried, evidently startled to see me. "And where would you be going this fine morn?"

The knowledge that even he was hard at work on the Lord's Day sent my spirits tumbling to my toes. "I was going to service," I told him, blinking back tears. "But I couldn't find the church."

"Oh, we don't need churches or churchmen

around here," he said, clapping me on the shoulder. "Every man his own priest these days, isn't that right? Look here, love, don't be so down in the mouth. I'll walk you back up the path. And master'll be here maybe today, that'll be grand, eh?"

As he set down his spade, he tipped the handle slightly so that the metal grip touched my arm, with a casual expression on his face, as if it were only an accident; but I knew it was more than that. I should have demanded what he meant by it, and what the village woman had meant by it, too, taking care to touch me with metal as though I were a witch or a fairy. But I was nothing but half grown then, and shy, and thought it impertinence to pry into the affairs of my elders.

We came to the front door, and I looked at the letters above it; many fine letters there were. "What does it say?" I asked.

"It says 'Seldom House'—that's the name of the place," he answered. "You'll excuse my leaving, young maid. I've work to finish before the master returns." And he set off whistling along the way we had come.

I stayed to scrutinize the letters above the door; some few of them I knew, and I thought I could tell

"House" plain enough, but it seemed to me that other words were carved there besides. Not for the first time did I wish I could read as I scanned the letters for shapes I knew, but though I worked on the puzzle for some time, none of it could I make out.

Not wishing to lose the good of that rare pleasant weather, and not wanting to go back into that dark house, I skirted the barnyard and climbed up into the pasture beneath the green ridge. There my spirits rose as the glorious day unfolded around me, and larks and lapwings darted and tumbled in the sky. And, remembering my friend the curate in the shadowless beyond, I held church on the hillside and sang with the birds as many joyful hymns as I could recall.

In a little hollow where the gusts didn't blow so strongly, I ate my bread and cheese and pillowed my head on a tuft to look for shapes in the slow-moving clouds. The monotonous bleating of the sheep, mixed with the higher-pitched cry of the lambs, and the rush of wind in the meadow grasses soon lulled me to sleep.

I did not wake until late afternoon, when the westering sun dropped behind the rocky crest, and it cast its cool shadow over me. Then I started up in confusion, thinking I had been remiss, and reproaching myself for making so free with my time, more like I had been gentry than servant.

When I opened the kitchen door, I found that I had been missed. Miss Winter came sweeping around the bare wooden table, demanding to know where I had been. She was in a state of high excitement, with color in her cheeks, and a tall, good-looking gentleman stood beside her.

"So this is the young maid," he exclaimed, bending down to greet me. "Flora, I can't tell if you're doing God's work or the devil's."

Miss Winter turned pink, then went pale. "That's not funny, Jack," she said.

He introduced himself as Jack Ketch; however, I learned soon enough that this was not his name, but rather the sort of joke he liked best. He had yellow hair and a yellow curling beard, and his eyes were large and gray. He was past his first youth and had reached an age when men are expected to act with dignity, but he seemed to me all the more agreeable for being so full of high spirits. I felt in my heart that his teasing comment had not been kind, but such was his charm that I found myself grinning all the same and shaking his hand gladly when he offered it.

"Are you ready to meet the master?" he asked me, eyebrows raised.

"I'm very pleased to meet you," I returned timidly.

This brought a howl of dismay from the hearth. "He's not the master—I am!"

A small boy hurtled out of a corner by the fire, where Mrs. Sexton had been working to undress him. He was perhaps six, but his face looked older, touched with hunger; he was sallow-skinned, with a shock of black hair hanging over his eyes. A dirtier child could not be imagined, and I drew away, mindful of my new dress.

"I'm the master!" yelped the little imp, his dark eyes daring me to disagree, while Mr. Ketch traded glances with Miss Winter, on the verge of laughter.

"Indeed you are," said Mr. Ketch, clapping the boy on the shoulder. "All that I have is yours, little man, and this house is only the beginning. And you're my shaggy godless devil, aren't you, you little heathen git?"

I blinked at the vulgarity, which tarnished Mr. Ketch's charm, but the little boy tilted his head back to view his hero and showed his sharp teeth in a smile. "I'm a heathen git!" he confirmed with vigor.

"And a little soap won't do you any harm," said Mr. Ketch, holding his neophyte off at arm's length.

"I'll thank you not to go smirching my clean breeches. Young master, this is your very own young maid, so shake hands. She's here to be your playmate. Now, go to Mrs. Sexton and let her make you presentable."

With that, he and Miss Winter left the kitchen, talking easily like old friends.

Mrs. Sexton set me stirring a turpentine concoction while she bathed the little boy in a tub. We had to change the water several times, lugging the tub between us, and I was vexed that the urchin splashed my new dress. "I'm master of this kitchen," he proclaimed when I scolded him. "Master of you, and you, and them in the other room."

"Is that gentleman his father?" I inquired of Mrs. Sexton, nodding towards the door through which Mr. Ketch had gone.

"You mean the old master?" she said. "I doubt it." And she dabbed the turpentine mixture on the boy to kill his lice.

"See here," I said to the little boy next, "is the old master your dad?"

"Him? Not likely," he answered, enduring the stinging concoction without complaint. "Old Jack paid a pretty penny to get me."

"Then you're nobody's master," I concluded

triumphantly. "Nobody makes a stranger's son the master of his land. He's just having you on."

He opened his eyes wide enough at that intelligence and made a swipe to get me. I dodged, and he upset the turpentine over the hearthstones, where it raised a stink to make all our eyes water. A soapy sponge came hurtling through the air next and slapped me on the side of the head. Only the arrival of Arnby at the kitchen door prevented further combat.

"Where's the young master?" he inquired respectfully, removing his hat. "Oh, there you are, young sir. Allow me to bid you welcome to your new home. I'm here to get you measured."

After Arnby left, Mrs. Sexton sat us down to our supper. The little boy crammed food into his mouth with both hands, glaring at me all the while like a famished dog.

"What's your name?" I asked, hoping to recall him to good manners, but my tactic didn't work. He only muttered gibberish, or some savage tongue, and leered at me when I looked baffled.

"My name's Tabby," I said, "and you'll have to call me that; I'll not answer otherwise. Now, this time tell me your name."

For answer, he said the same gibberish as before

and repeated it so readily and so often that I was forced to conclude it must be a designation of some sort; but on no account could I say it or remember it, no matter how often he jabbered it out.

"Don't you have a Christian name?" I asked. "What does Mr. Ketch call you?"

"He calls me his rogue, or his little heathen git," answered the boy, snatching my last crust of bread from me.

"Well, I won't call you any such thing," I asserted, resigning the crumb with dignity. "You'll have to have a decent Christian name." But this sent my companion into a torrent of gibberish, laughing all the while over my annoyance.

"Bed," grunted Mrs. Sexton, rising from her bench and laying aside her pipe. That put me in mind of the cold dead girl who waited to share my bed with me.

Before I could speak, my problem settled itself. "I want to sleep with her," clamored the little boy with the heathen name. "Her room is mine, isn't it, so she has to let me."

I acquiesced at once.

Almost immediately, I repented my decision. Upon reaching our room, the little boy skinned up a bedpost and swarmed about in the curtains, shouting commands to himself about rigging and sails. I expected Mrs. Sexton to order him down, but she went about her work at the hearth as if she were deaf and dumb.

"Come down from there before you tear the fabric," I demanded in as imperious a manner as I knew, but he hung upside down from the canopy frame and laughed at my attempt at authority.

"I don't do what you want," he replied. "I'm master here."

"Then act like one. Masters don't go climbing about in the bed curtains."

To my surprise, that remark worked on him like magic. "What do masters do?" he asked soberly, dropping to the floor. When I informed him that masters lay down, said their prayers, and went to sleep, he surprised me again by his compliance. "No prayers, though," he told me. "Old Master Jack don't say them."

We soon were tucked in as well as could be expected, though he stank horribly of turpentine and squirmed like a litter of puppies. The phlegmatic Mrs. Sexton took her leave, locking the door behind her.

I had been afraid of the coming night, but this night was nothing like before. My companion played

noisy games with the shadows on the curtains, nar-
rating pretend combats. I had no thought to spare
for ghosts then; it took all my ingenuity to deal with
the living. But I hit upon the strategy of asking my
charge to name all the things of which he was
master. The result was an exhaustive reckoning, and
a capital soporific: I held on through a long list
of pots, pans, crockery, and fire irons, but dozed off
while he was naming the butter churn, the back
stairs, and all the jam in the pantry.

When he jerked upright, he startled me. I
opened my eyes to find the firelight gone and the
room completely dark.

"Get away!" he cried. "We don't want you here.
You can't come in!"

"What is the matter?" I asked in confusion,
reaching out to quiet him. "Wisht now, you're having a nightmare."

"No nightmare," he said decisively. "It was some
girl sneaking into bed. I sent her away. Lucky for
you I let you stay here," he added, snuggling close
to me.

In an instant, he was asleep again, breathing
deeply and evenly, while I lay awake and wondered
if I had imagined the sound of footsteps running
away.

CHAPTER FOUR

LIVELY DISARRAY met my gaze when I climbed out of bed in the morning: my companion had discovered the childish treasure in the bottom of the clothes press and had scattered it across the floor. The papers were trodden on, a sampler was covered in ashes, and most of the feathers were spoiled, for he was using them as swords to fight a duel, stabbing the air, with shouts and curses.

"Hush your noise," I said, gathering up the items to restore them to their hiding place. He paused to watch me, chest heaving, probably considering the best way to run me through. Then his sword became a feather again, and he dropped it to the floor for me to tidy up with the others.

"What did you wrap the mirror for?" I wanted to know. He had draped it with a pillowcase.

"It's no good," he answered, heaping the buttons into a pile. "When I look in, other faces look out."

"It's old," I said. "It needs new silver." But all the same, I didn't unwrap it.

"It's where the other girl lives," he said, sitting on the floor and setting the coins on their edges like wheels. "She can't live in the chimney, her fingers wouldn't be so cold then."

"She's dead," I told him. "She can pass through the locked door."

He rolled one of the coins into his pile of buttons. "Dead people creep into the house at night," he said, "to hunt for crumbs under the table."

I shuddered, then pretended it was due to the chilly morning and dragged a blanket from the press to pull around my shoulders. "That's a foolish, pagan idea," I said, sitting down beside him. "The dead do no such thing. The bad dead go to hell and roast in flames, and the good dead go to the kingdom of heaven and sing songs with the Lord Jesus."

"*She* didn't go anywhere," he said, aiming another coin at his stack.

"Maybe she did," I rejoined virtuously. "Maybe she's come visiting. She'll do us no harm. A curate told me the dead can't harm the living."

"What's a curate?" he wanted to know.

I was deeply shocked. "How could you not know that? They preach, and christen babies, and marry people, and when you die they follow your casket and pray over the grave."

"They must know about dead people, then," admitted the little boy.

After breakfast, my charge was restless indoors, possessed with a keen desire to climb onto a sideboard and pluck down one of the weapons that hung as decoration above it: a reasonable course, he did not tire of telling me, as they belonged to no one else. To discourage his martial zeal, I persuaded him to walk with me in a private garden that lay next to the house, though the sky was lowering and the wind was chill. This garden I had seen through the windows of Miss Winter's room, and I had spotted its high walls while I was up on the hillside the day before.

Once there, I discovered I didn't like it. The high rock walls gave us shelter, but the north wind whistled and moaned in their cracks. It was a topiary garden; but while the general form of such plantings is orderly and geometric, with neat hedges and cunning shapes, this had become overgrown, and its present gardeners had no interest in restoring order or design. The yew bushes were enormous, taller than a grown man's head, and clipped into irregular, bulbous shapes, like huge dark puddings.

There I learned that the mind is unhappy with uncertainty and tries to make sense of the senseless. The yews seemed to my mind like giants huddled in dark cloaks, fat men with wide hats, stacks of millstones, or heaps of boulders. So far were they from their original size that we had to turn sideways to edge past their unnatural forms. Their effect within the enclosed space was suffocating.

My companion, being smaller, didn't mind as much as I. To him, they were ideal barricades from which to prepare an ambush for the enemy, a fallen twig supplying him with a gun and another becoming a knife. He ran and shouted, collected spiders and executed them with great cruelty and solemnity, and amused himself for an hour with little assistance from me.

At length, he tired of vigorous pursuits and settled in a mossy corner where garden wall met house wall and the monster yews drew back a pace. Here he set to building a dungeon scooped out of the mold, and for prisoners, peopling it with earthworms.

It vexed me that he had no name, so I sat by while he played and tried out all the names I knew. None of them seemed to suit him. They matched healthy English boys who played ball on the village green. My charge was assuredly not English, with his sallow face and gibbering speech; in play, he lapsed again and again into his barbarous tongue. Like a fairy-tale beast that required a special word to tame it, he required a name beyond the ones I knew.

"Do you know what name you were christened by?" I ventured to ask, but his ignorance on the point was so profound that he had doubtless never been christened at all. Then superstition took hold, and I began to fear I would be naming him for the first time, and thus become responsible for his fate. There is a witchcraft in names. They are not a trifling matter.

"I'm a heathen git," he proclaimed with satisfaction. "That's my Christian name."

"Don't be vulgar," I said. "You don't know what that means."

"Can you tie a hitch?" he asked, picking up a

twig, and he proceeded to demonstrate the art with one of the prisoner worms. This interested me: it was something like knitting, so I entered into the play. Before long, he had progressed in his instruction, and I could splice a brace of worms as neatly as any sailor. I repaid him by demonstrating the best love knot I knew; but here our resources failed us and we had to go digging again, for the love knot required many worms.

I began to grow uneasy. I could feel a person's gaze, and yet no one was there. I supposed Miss Winter walked in the garden, for now and then I thought I caught a flash of black dress between the shapes of yew. But I could not be sure. The day was drear, and the tall bushes rose like slabs of dark rock to block my line of sight.

"Untie the short one there, I'll add it to the end," directed Himself. This was the title I had bestowed on him in my mind for the purpose of avoiding a name.

I caught movement at the corner of my eye a few feet off in the garden. Black dress. Black sockets. The dead maid. But the instant I saw her, she vanished.

"What do I do after this turn?" he asked. "Hi! Don't scoot there, you'll mash the end."

Just at the edge of my vision, she walked by again. I scooted further, ignoring his curses. "I don't like facing the corner, that's all."

We were playing by the slender trunk of a short exotic tree, with long thin leaves clustered like a child's fingers. I turned my back to the tree and to our corner, facing down the crowd of formless shrubs. A gust of wind blew the little leaf hands down to tickle the back of my neck. One of the hands was ice cold.

"Let's go inside," I said, jumping up and accidentally treading on our knot.

Himself continued tying worms. "You're doing what he wants," he told me. "Act like you don't see him."

"Who?" I asked, turning from side to side in my agitation.

"The old man with eyes like windows."

Black cloth flashed between the yews, but this time Mr. Ketch came through the dark green shapes, dressed in a sober suit of dull black twill. He cut a fine figure, but his handsome face had lost its color and fallen into lines. Our worm knots set him laughing, and he resumed his accustomed appearance.

"How's my little heathen git?" he demanded,

and the sallow-faced boy answered him with a joyful shout.

"Sir, do you know his name?" I asked.

Mr. Ketch clapped his protégé on the shoulders and gave him a playful shake. "A young rogue like this doesn't need a name, do you? Young rogue, I hate this house. I most particularly hate this garden. What do you say to a little shooting out on the moor?"

Himself shouted louder. Mr. Ketch glanced behind me and hurriedly looked away. "Good, good," he said. "Let's be gone. God, what a place for the nerves." And he marched Himself off so quickly that I couldn't keep up with them, though I had no liking for the garden either.

I whiled away the afternoon with Mrs. Sexton in the kitchen, helping her put the marks on a new set of sheets. We neither of us said ten words to the other and so got on capitally, for I'm not one to mix talk and work, and Mrs. Sexton was not one to talk at all. When we heard the shots, I thanked the Almighty that our bench was no closer to the window. I wouldn't have put a gun in that boy's hands for gold.

Arnby brought Himself into the kitchen some time later, the pair of them wearing long faces.

"The young master's not to go shooting," he told me, "nor do aught else that could be dangerous. Maidie, I expect you to see to it. Keep weapons out of his hands. And just look, young sir, it's started raining. You'd be coming inside regardless. We've got your health to think of, haven't we?"

This did little to mend matters with Himself, who retreated behind that shaggy black forelock of his and glowered like a thundercloud. He held his peace while Arnby stood by, but he made me leave my sewing, and when we had gained the passage-way, he gave full vent to his spleen. Old Master Jack and he had been having a grand time shooting birds when Arnby had come rushing up the hill. Then he and Master Jack had had a talk, and that was the end of the fun.

I came in for a share of his bad humor when I pointed out that spring was no time for shooting, as the birds were still raising their young. "I've a right to do as I please on my land," he exclaimed furiously. "I can shoot an egg if I want to!"

We were near Miss Winter's rooms just then, in a passage with homely rag rugs, one of the few passages in the house lit by its own window. This pleased me better than the dusty rooms upstairs, so we took it over for our play, Himself running and sliding on the rugs while I sat by on the stairs. Then he hit upon the plan of searching the house for objects of treasure—"loot" was his curious word for it.

"We'll take it to our room," he said. "I'm the leader, but we'll go share and share alike."

I thought this an excellent plan: it had the advantage of keeping us indoors and my charge out of harm's way. If he truly were master, as they all feigned, he could arrange the household goods as he liked, and if he weren't master, then this "loot" scheme would bring a swift end to the farce. Either way, we would learn a thing or two worth knowing.

The first room we searched was small and devoted primarily to books, which stood by the dozens in neat rows behind the glass of two mahogany cases. Several pictures of dull landscapes hung on the walls, and three large Dutch plates of blue and white reclined in a rack above a fruitwood chest of drawers.

A horse's hoof shod with a brass plate stood upon one of the bookcases. It struck my companion's fancy, but I pronounced it barbaric. A teapot with a bright scene painted on its side sat upon a small table next to a comb-backed chair. I should have liked to call it loot, but Himself refused, paying me in kind for dismissing his hoof.

He tried the drawers, but they were locked. Then he examined the right-hand bookcase, which was not. He took out a book, turning it various ways, and his eyebrows shot up when it opened.

"It's like a box," he said, tipping it upside down and fanning out the covers. "It holds things." But his voice was doubtful.

"Books hold words," I said, turning it over so we could see the pages. "These marks are all words. See, there's A. That's a word."

"Why keep old words?" he wondered. "Cannot you make new ones?"

"People write down words so that others can read them later," I said. "Like the name of this house over the door, or names on tombstones. Then the passersby can see if they knew that person, or if they're a relative. I know how to spell my name, Aykroyd, and I look for it when I pass graveyards."

"So a dead person did this?" asked Himself, growing interested.

A slight sound distracted us. Miss Winter stood in the doorway, with a countenance that made me wish I were elsewhere. Perhaps the loot plan was a bad one after all.

"I see you've had enough of polishing the hall floor," she remarked.

"We're taking loot," Himself told her. "Share and share alike."

"Then you may leave. I've no grace to squander on a pair of urchins rifling through my things."

"They're *my* things," retorted Himself. "If you ask for them, I'll give them back."

Miss Winter bestowed a tight smile on him. "Yes, the master owns everything, don't you? How gracious to give me my things. And what do you have there, master?"

"It's a box to put words in," he said. "Dead people's words."

Miss Winter laughed at him. "Admit that you don't know what it is. Fine possessions won't help you if you're too stupid to know what to do with them."

Himself stiffened, and his black eyes blazed. I thought he meant to strike her. But he tore out a handful of pages instead and hurled the book into the grate. While Miss Winter knelt to pluck it from the ashes, he ripped the loose pages into fragments. He said, "I knew what to do with that one, at any rate."

I expected her to box his ears at once for his rudeness and the ears of his nursemaid into the bargain. But when Miss Winter turned from the hearth, she still smiled, though it was an unpleasant smile, to be sure. "A good master wastes nothing," she declared. "He knows each object has a use. But a fool doesn't bother with what he knows nothing about, and that's what you are—a fool."

I thought this speech no harsher than her usual way, but her words struck their intended target. Himself flushed deep red. Eyes averted, he dropped the ragged slips of paper and quitted the chamber at a run. He pattered down one passageway and up another to the broad staircase of the entrance hall; then he charged up it and disappeared into a room at the top.

The chamber's only furnishing was a massive oak buffet. I arrived to find one of the cabinet doors standing open, and Himself crawling inside. "Come out," I coaxed, kneeling by his hiding place. "We'll play a better game." But he made no answer, nor did he speak thereafter, though I made the offer more than once.

The chamber, poor in furnishings, was rich in decoration, and I had leisure to study it while I knelt in the dust and made my entreaties. Painted leather panels covered the walls, displaying curling vines and bold flourishes of fanciful red and blue flowers. A raised pattern of interlaced circles enlivened the white plaster ceiling, and a carved wooden over-mantel surrounded the stone fireplace.

While sufficient daylight entered the diamond-paned window, the painted panels gleamed with mellow warmth. But as the low dark clouds thick-ened and rain beat against the panes, color leached out of the chamber. The painted flowers began to look like winter's withered leaves, and the molded ceiling like a frozen pond etched by the blades of skaters. Twilight gathered in the corners, and the rich details melted into the gloom. The heavy carv-ing of the overmantel, muffled in dust, seemed to writhe with voluptuous shapes. Stains on the leather panels took on sinister forms.

"Boy! Come out now," I begged. "I'm cold, and I want my tea."

Himself made no answer.

A point of darkness flickered at the edge of my vision—the shadow, as it were, of a candle flame. Frightened, I squinted at the square door of the buffet, determined not to take notice. The point thickened and spread, blocking the light from the window. A black dress next to my black dress. Gray hands reaching for mine.

With a shriek, I dove inside the cabinet, surpris-ing the little boy who huddled there. "Shift yourself!"

he ordered, shoving at me. "You're treading on my legs."

"It's her!" I cried. "It's her. If she comes in here, I think I'll die."

"Who? Old Miss Wheyface?"

"Wisht! Wisht!" Then I had to battle with myself to take my own advice.

We held our breath, but even the wind was quiet. Not so much as a creak of old timber did we hear.

"The ghost girl," I whispered to Himself. "She stood right beside me."

He leaned past me to push the door open and looked out into the room. "I don't see her," he remarked, evidently disappointed. "And you told me this morning the dead do no harm."

His words put me in mind of the curate who had spoken them, himself now dead and gone. Ghosts shouldn't frighten us, he had said, but I could not shake my dread of this one. She seemed so ghastly, trying to touch me with those dead hands, as if we were old friends. What reason did she have to seek me out?

I crept from the buffet into the gloom of the coming night. A hand touched mine, and I jumped, but it was only Himself who stood beside me.

"Time for tea," I said, pulling him to the stairs. "Tea, and a nice hot fire."

Deep in the nighttime, when not a spark gleamed indoors, nor a star without, the dead maid stood by my bedside again and summoned me from sleep. She shook me as if to rouse me and take me with her, those chilly fingers sliding down my arm; I could not move for sheer terror, but shrank within myself. Then the little boy beside me stirred in the darkness, and his breath blew warm on my face. Breath, warmth, life—and courage.

"Go away!" I cried. "We don't want you here!" The icy fingers released me, and I sat up in bed. "Go away! You mean nothing to me. I don't know you, you're dead, go away!"

This time, I heard no footsteps, but I could feel that she had fled.

"The ghost girl?" asked Himself quite calmly as I lay back down, and I marveled that such a young child did not cry.

When day broke, I found two altogether ordinary objects resting on the pillow beside me. So ordinary were they, in fact, that at first I gave them no notice. Two socks, of exactly the sort I had made every day for the past year or more. One sock had come from the hiding place in the clothes press, I discovered, and the other had come out of my great-coat pocket. It was the sock I had been working during my journey to the house—had begun, but never finished. Yet here it was, tied off and complete, in the style of Ma Hutton's school.

And then I knew who the dead maid was.

CHAPTER FIVE

WHEN MRS. SEXTON unlocked our door, I was waiting for her. "What happened to Izzy?" I demanded.

She set down the ash bucket and handed me black clothes. "For the young master," she said. "Took long enough, they were letting out the old master's things first."

Himself was solemn as I helped him out of his rags and dressed him. "Master Jack wears a black coat," he observed, twisting to try to see the back of his outfit.

I felt proud of my charge. The new clothes suited his dark coloring and made him look a handsome lad; and then, he had that bearing some people have, even at his young age, of being the one who ought to be giving the orders.

"He's still barefoot," I observed. "With a coat like this, he needs stockings and leather shoes."

Mrs. Sexton was running a rag over the mantel. "Nay, he's all right," she said.

"And why black?" I wanted to know. "You don't wear it." Her own dress was brown homespun.

"Black's just for family," she muttered.

The absurdity of this remark loosened my tongue, and high time for it too. "But we're *not* family," I protested. "We none of us are. I've never worked in a house with more awkward staffing. And what *did* happen to Izzy? She came from the same school I did, and she wore black even though she wasn't family. She should be a young woman by now. Instead, she's walking nights. Why? The dead walk for a reason."

Mrs. Sexton cleared away the ashes and laid on the new coals. Then she sat back on her heels. "She was a sweet little thing. Didn't know she was called Izzy. I don't learn their names."

"Who killed her?" demanded Himself, standing

by her on the hearth, an odd caricature of respectability in his fine black suit and bare feet. "Tell us who killed her. I want to watch him hang."

Mrs. Sexton took her pipe from her belt and cleaned out its bowl into the ash bucket. "You'll have to ask the old maid or master that, young sir. I'm not one to tell tales."

We ran downstairs to breakfast, hearing as we went the hiss of raindrops against glass panes and the gentle plash of water dripping into shallow puddles in distant chambers of the house. When we reached the kitchen, we found a gray torrent pelting against the large windows, and the tall bushes by the garden wall bending and twitching under its onslaught as though they shuddered from the cold. There would be no chance of a ramble today, I told myself as we ate our bowls of porridge, and I contemplated the unwelcome prospect of amusing my high-spirited charge indoors.

"Old Miss Wheyface will be in her rooms," the little boy observed. "You can ask her what happened to your friend." Then he appropriated my porridge and started in on it while I contemplated the even more unwelcome prospect of attempting to interrogate Miss Winter.

After breakfast, I followed him to Miss Winter's

chambers, rather wishing I were going elsewhere. Miss Winter sat on a sofa with a tea tray nearby, her finger marking her place in a book. She winced as we entered hand in hand.

"Lovely day for a funeral," she said.

"It's the clothes Mrs. Sexton ordered for us," I explained, brushing crumbs from Himself's coat. He responded by pushing me away scornfully and advancing out of my reach. "Mrs. Sexton says black's just for family," I continued.

"So it is," she said.

"But we're not family," I pointed out.

"Indeed you are not," she replied.

"But that makes no sense."

"No, it doesn't," she agreed, turning back to her book. "Is that all?"

It almost was. Miss Winter was exerting her usual influence over me. I could feel myself growing ugly and stupid. My companion diverted my attention by picking up a costly teacup. "The dead girl," he prompted when I signaled him to put it down.

"He means Izzy, miss," I said as she glanced up sharply. "I—we, that is—we think it's her, and we believe she's not at rest. Mrs. Sexton told us to ask you about it."

"Izzy." Miss Winter's brow dented, and she

pursed her lips. "Izzy . . . she was the first girl from your establishment, is that right?"

"Yes, miss," I responded.

"She died not long ago. She visits me too. I don't think she wants to leave. She was so happy here."

"Happy, miss?" I asked in some confusion. It wasn't that I couldn't picture a girl wanting to linger where she had been happy. It was that I couldn't picture it happening here.

"I blame myself," said Miss Winter. "She was a pretty thing, and I made a pet of her. I haven't been myself since she died. Perhaps if I could stop thinking of her, she would rest."

She went on like that, talking of the times they had had together, a lonely woman and her maid. Himself soon tired of listening and wandered off into the next room. Miss Winter didn't seem to be listening to herself, either, and that distracted me; it made me wonder what she was thinking of just then, and I looked for signs of it. That handsome white face of hers never varied by much; it showed only what she wanted it to show. But her eyes showed too much, flashing and gleaming, roaming the room as if she wished I were gone.

In her tale, Izzy was growing ill. Too much indulgence, weak lungs, a delicate constitution.

Delicate like the fine porcelain teacup, I thought. That was what Miss Winter's face resembled: delicate white plates. Expensive, perfect. Brittle.

"We shared everything," Miss Winter said, shaking her head sadly. "She was like the sister I never had."

"Like your own child, miss?" I asked sympathetically.

"No!"

Her glittering eyes transfixed me with a baleful glare. They gave me quite a turn. In one of my houses, the grandmother had lost her wits, and they had kept her tied to a chair. I should have liked Miss Winter to be tied to a chair just then.

Gradually, her eyes dimmed, and she composed herself.

"Yes, I suppose so," she sighed. "I suppose she was like . . . like you say. Family. And you see now why you aren't family yet, even though you're dressed like family. But perhaps one day soon we'll call each other sister."

I could envision no stretch of time long enough to produce such an unnerving result. "Yes, miss. Thank you, miss," I answered. "I'd best see what the young one is up to." And I made my escape, deeply grateful that Miss Winter was not yet prepared to take to her heart another sister she had never had.

"Tabby, come see what I've found," called Himself in a conspiratorial tone, crouching next to an open drawer.

Inside lay two wax dolls as long as my forearm, crudely fashioned out of candle-tallow. They had neither hair nor clothes, and nothing but the merest hint of features, but we could tell one was a man and the other a woman. The dolls were run through and through with steel pins until they bristled with shining metal.

I spied in the bottom of the drawer the enameled miniature of a lovely young woman with fair hair, rosy lips, and round white arms—the lid, or so it appeared, of a gentleman's snuff box. But, alas! it had been ruined, wrenched from its box and then smashed, so that cracks disfigured the charming face and white flakes wreathed it round, instead of lace. Beside the lid lay a lock of yellow hair, of such a hue and curl that I perceived it must have belonged to Mr. Ketch.

"This one's mine," whispered Himself as he snatched up the man. "You can have her if you want." And we tiptoed into the passage with our treasures, careful lest Miss Winter see us taking loot.

In my whole life, I had had but one doll, a simple wooden dowel with a face of ink, and that humble creature had come to a violent end, chewed by the head groom's mastiff. Now I carried my poor injured wax figure to the kitchen and promised the straight pins to Mrs. Sexton for a candle end, whose flame I used to aid their removal and smooth the wounds left behind. I named my new plaything Alma Augusta after a rich girl I had once served, because she had had fair hair like the pretty woman in the smashed portrait. Why this fancy seized me, I cannot tell; my bald and battered Alma bore scant resemblance to the fair-haired stranger, except that both had been badly treated.

Taking an interest in our play, Mrs. Sexton fetched her rag basket and let us choose scraps to clothe them. Himself refused my offer to make proper garments for his doll. Instead, he knotted a piece of cloth around its legs in an ingenious fashion so that it looked like a baby's clout. Nor would he allow me to remove the steel pins that pierced his doll's bare chest.

"Mine's a pirate," he told me. "They shot him full of arrows, but he can't be killed. He's the most frightening pirate, sailors drown themselves before he captures them because he makes them die terrible ways."

"Wouldn't he rather be a lord?" I suggested, thinking that he would make rough company for Alma Augusta.

"He *is* a lord," said Himself, waving the figure menacingly at my young lady doll, who retired modestly behind a piece of cloth. "He's a lord because he took over a whole island and killed all the natives, and now he lives in a palace and they call him Lord."

"King, I should think," I corrected him.

"Lord Pirate," he declared. "Because he's the most evil pirate in the world."

"And what's his name?" I asked casually. I had a plan, you see. This pirate's character seemed an accurate portrait of my bloodthirsty young charge, and I had high hopes his name might serve a double purpose.

Himself grew quiet to ponder this, and his pirate grew quiet as well. Then he waved the scarred warrior around in a great flourish.

"Rogue!" he shouted. "That's his name, Lord Pirate Rogue."

And so my cunning plan came to nothing.

A piece of patterned chintz in the basket caught my eye, white flowers with a background of red. I soon had it cut into pieces and basted together. As I sewed the tiny seams, I hummed to myself, admiring my choice. The bold pattern was just the thing for a confident, adventurous lady. She should have petticoats, though, and if I didn't mind the work, I could make a band of lace to edge them. Ma Hutton had taught us a simple pattern. Setting the dress aside, I rummaged in the rag basket for a piece of bleached muslin to serve as undergarments.

When I turned back not a minute later, I found my doll's dress stuck fast to the kitchen table. A forest of straight pins transfixed the white flowers, skewering them to the wood beneath. I caught my breath and felt myself grow dizzy.

"Did you do this?" I asked Himself when I could speak, although I knew he hadn't. He had been sitting cross-legged before the fire, shouting orders while his pirate flogged a company of twigs. Now he rose and trotted over to the table to see.

"Pull them out, Tabby. I can't," he complained. "They've been driven in with a hammer."

Mrs. Sexton fetched pincers and soon wrenched them out.

"I didn't do it," I told her as she gathered them up.

She answered, "I never said you did."

I went back to my sewing, sick at heart now, with all the joy gone out of the task. Himself crouched on the hearth, whispering to himself or to his pirate in his play. Mrs. Sexton bent her head over her mending. By degrees, the room grew quiet.

I felt someone lean over me, but a quick glance found nothing.

"Come play," ordered Himself from the hearth. "My pirate wants to meet your lady. She can be his third wife."

A presence behind me made my skin crawl with its nearness. "My lady won't have him," I snapped.

"He'll run her through with his sword then. What do you keep looking at?"

"Nothing!" And nothing it was. My nerves sang like plucked strings.

"You're poorly," declared Mrs. Sexton, setting down her mending. She went to the pantry to fetch me a mug of milk. But when I reached for it, invisible fingers clutched the handle. I shoved it from me and jumped to my feet.

"It's her!" I cried, stumbling from the table.

"No, it's him," said Himself, pointing at the ground.

The spilled milk had puddled on the slate floor

in the shape of a thin white face, with two dark slate circles for eyes and a round empty O for the mouth. We stood in a body and stared down at it.

"It's the old man," said Himself. "He smells bad, and he yells at me. He was just here."

Stunned, I appealed to the busy housekeeper, who was on her knees mopping up the face. "Mrs. Sexton, is there another ghost?"

"The dead master? Oh, aye," she said. "He'll not rest easy at a time like this. Such a temper he had on him, and it grew worse before the end. There's times I thought he'd throttle the life from me for letting his bread fall."

Feeling ill, I sat down at the table. Himself seemed subdued too. He leaned against me and began playing with Alma Augusta's red dress.

"What happened to the old man?" he wanted to know.

"Had an attack," said Mrs. Sexton. "Apoplexy or some such. There's rules to this house. Master can't be an invalid."

"But what if he is?"

"He isn't for long."

She replaced the spilled milk, then laid another coal on the fire and resumed her seat. I gingerly reached for the mug, secured its handle, and shared its contents with my young charge.

"Master Jack would be the old man's son, then," I guessed.

"I'll say not!" Mrs. Sexton pursed her lips in a grimace. "A right fine time those two will have when they're together at last."

"Then I can't make it out at all, at all," I told her, spreading my hands in an appeal for reason. "How is it Master Jack's master now if he wasn't the old master's son?"

Mrs. Sexton's unexpected chattiness dried up. She closed her teeth around her pipe with an audible snap. For several minutes, she stared into the fire, puffing, until curls of smoke surrounded her. Then, just when we thought to hear no more from her, she spoke.

"In most houses, family's related by birth. Seldom House family's related by death." And that was all she would say.

My young charge seemed to take meaning away from the riddle that changed his conduct for the worse. When Mr. Ketch came into the kitchen not long thereafter, Himself was decidedly cool. He went on directing the battle his twigs were waging to claim the coal scuttle for their lord and ignored Mr. Ketch's jokes and blandishments. As Mrs. Sexton didn't bother to speak, either, I felt the obligation descend upon me.

"Are you ill, sir?" I inquired. The clear response was *yes*. Jack Ketch's countenance was sickly yellow, almost a match for his beard.

"Not at all, I'm fit for a wager," he answered with an attempt at a grin. "So, heathen git! What's the game then?"

Himself went on playing.

"He's not well either, sir," I interjected when I saw the man's hurt expression. "A ghost in this house threatens him."

I expected raised eyebrows or a hearty laugh, but Mr. Ketch shivered and quickly scanned the room, then turned up his collar and drew his coat close as though he stood outside in the cold drizzle. "You'd think they'd leave children in peace," he sighed.

"The boy is in peril," I made bold to add. "It's no surprise he's surrounded by evil spirits when he's still in thrall to the devil. We owe it to him to see him christened and set on the right path."

"Oh, ah!" exclaimed Mr. Ketch, and now he seemed amused. "You're an old-fashioned little body, aren't you? But we've no parson here, so your righteous plan will take some doing." He gave a start, glanced behind himself at nothing, and made for the door.

"You might do it yourself, sir," I pointed out, but he was past hearing.

For the next hour, not a single twig was whipped or burnt at the stake, and by this I could see that my charge's mind was not on his play. But we scarcely could have dreamt what that barbaric little thing was up to. When Mrs. Sexton reached down the earthenware plates for our tea, he surprised us both.

"I'm master, and old Jack's master," he said. "That's a joke, though, isn't it? It's like the Lord Pirate Rogue, there can't be more than one."

"I told you that days ago," I said primly.

"I thought so. I'll have to kill him," he said, quite calm. "He's bigger than I am. There'll be lots of blood."

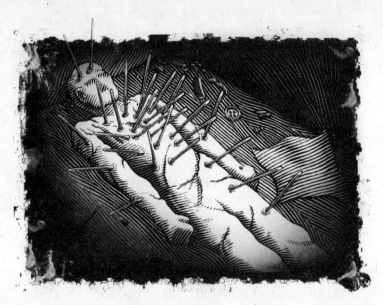

CHAPTER SIX

I HAVE NEVER been squeamish, but I thought I might faint, hearing a small child speak so about murder.

"Don't be ridiculous!" I snapped. "That wild talk is fine for your wax doll, but this is a civilized land. You'll end up on the gallows if you go on raving like that. Gentlemen don't kill one another. Do they, Mrs. Sexton?"

But that grim lady gave a puff on her pipe and turned away to fetch our meal.

"How else do they get land, then?" Himself asked, as cool as you please.

"They wait, and they inherit it. That's what Mr. Ketch did. After all he's done for you, to say such a thing! I wonder he doesn't send you about your business."

He seemed half inclined to believe me, though a trifle disappointed. I honestly think the little savage would have liked to try his scheme.

"Old Jack don't act like a master," he retorted. "I'd not do as he bids."

"Of course he acts like a master," I said. "He does as he pleases, that's what masters do. Have you seen him out hoeing the fields?"

"Masters sit at the head of the table with their people around them, all watching to do as they're told," he replied. "And masters give the orders like Arnby does. Jack doesn't do it, he runs away and hides even from me, and he's scared all the time now. He acts like a sneaky dog."

He jumped up from the hearth and faced Mrs. Sexton.

"If I'm master, I won't have my food in here like you do," he told her. "I'll sit at the head of the table and make old Jack come to me. Then we'll see which one is master."

"Masters don't act so," I argued. "Not when they're little. You're not fit to leave the nursery!"

But Mrs. Sexton was already returning the humble earthenware plates to their places.

"Supper in the dining room, then," she said. "I'll see to it, young sir." And she crossed the passage to another room, from whence we heard the clink of dishes. It upset me terribly to see her coddle him so.

"Now, you go fetch old Jack," he said, turning to me.

"I won't do it," I said, standing with my hands behind my back. "I've had enough of your heathen airs and threats, and I'm not going to humor you further." I was resolved, if he came at me, to turn him over my knee.

But the little imp was smarter than that.

"Don't be angry with me, Tabby," he said, putting his arms around my waist, and I swear he knew what it meant to me to hear my name, since no one else in that godforsaken house would use it. "Mrs. Sexton doesn't mind. Why should you? Go find him now, I know you like to see him."

I said *no* to that and more, and I argued and

grumbled besides, but in the end I found myself walking the hallways, searching for Mr. Ketch.

Voices issued from behind the closed door of Miss Winter's parlor. I leaned in close and ascertained that one of them was his. I had already lifted my hand to knock when I heard Miss Winter say, "Please, Jack. No one needs to know."

Now, it's a wicked thing when staff listen at doors, and I'll be the first to say it. But in that disordered place, with nothing but riddles to go on, and the whole house at sixes and sevens, I am not ashamed to say that I listened as if I had two sets of ears.

"Just a little money," she begged, "enough to set me up on my own, and you'd never have to see my face again. They don't need a maid, you know that. Arnby says it's the master who counts."

"And ruin the luck?" Mr. Ketch's voice was indignant. "You've damaged it enough already, trying to run off with the coal merchant. The *Annabelle Jacobs* sank that very week, and all our cargo with her. You know what investments mean to this estate. We're not getting rich off the village. Those clods pay their rent in potatoes and corn!"

"You're rich enough to lose five ships, I know

you are," she said. "They tell me how you live. As for the luck, I don't give two pins about that. I wish this house and its village and all its luck were gone from the face of the earth."

"You were glad enough when we found this place," Mr. Ketch returned. "You danced through the halls with your hair down."

"I hate it just as much as you do now, and you know perfectly well why. I'm begging you, Jackie. Just do this one thing for me, please."

"And let you out to come creeping down alleys after me?" His tone was snide. "That's all I need, my old friend Flora skulking and spying on me."

"I know you won't believe it possible," rejoined Miss Winter. "Your powers of imagination will be taxed to the utmost. But I don't care to spy on you. I don't love you anymore."

I heard a loud thump and started back, but it was only him rising from his chair and dropping something, or perhaps throwing it to the floor.

"Love!" I heard him shout as he paced the room with rapid strides. "Is that what they call it in your grand books of poetry when a woman leaves her baby in the cradle to run off with a boy of sixteen? Love!" He gave a snort. "I know some other pretty names for it."

"I didn't do so badly by you, Jackie," she cried. "Those early years were good years, when we'd found this place and the money came pouring in. The luck of Seldom House came true for us, didn't it, and we were as happy as two people ever could be.

"I know about her, the fair-haired girl," she continued, and her voice shook as she said it. "She's lovely, Jackie. Really quite lovely. I know that's why you sent me home, but I'm not angry, truly. Just remember the good times like I do. Give me this one thing now."

"Her? You mean them!" His laughter was harsh. "I've lost count, there've been so many, and every one of them was better than you, with your jealous moods and mad rages. What about poor little Evie, who ended up in the mill race for kissing me at the harvest dance? No, I'll not let you out to roam the countryside; it's a public duty to keep you confined."

At first, only harsh and irregular breaths answered him. Then Miss Winter mastered herself and spoke, her voice strangled and harsh.

"Evie drowned herself," she said. "I was miles away, and you know it. It suits your precious vanity to pretend I'd do murder for your sake, but listen to me, little Jack Cookson, you puling mamma's darling, I feel nothing but pity for those silly girls who waste their days buttoning your breeches and wiping your chin. And I'd not leave now if you begged me to. I wouldn't miss the show. It warms my heart to think that one day I'll watch you die, and we'll always have each other then, Jackie boy."

"You damned witch!" he shrieked. "Why, I'll watch you die right now!" And from within the room came the sound of crashing furniture. I did not stay to listen while they killed each other, but ran away in fright.

Himself stood in the doorway of a handsome dining room, with Chinese plates and crystal glasses set upon the table, and tapers shining in the brackets. Mrs. Sexton brought a tureen from the kitchen, and I turned to help her. He stood by to watch us work, like proper gentry.

"Well?" he asked when he saw me alone.

"I couldn't disturb them," I said.

Mrs. Sexton looked me over, and she must have guessed what had occurred. "I'll disturb them," she said grimly.

She soon returned with the unholy pair. Their eyes were flashing, and their color was high, and not a word did they say while we sat on padded chairs and Mrs. Sexton served the soup. But after supper was over and Mr. Ketch had stormed off to cool his temper in some other corner of the house, Miss Winter sipped wine by the fireside quite peacefully and watched the two of us play.

"What do you have there?" she asked Himself.

Now, I had had the good sense to leave Alma Augusta in the kitchen, but Himself was playing with the other wax doll right in front of her. He trotted over and showed her his plaything, bristling with pins and scars.

"He's a pirate," proclaimed Himself.

To my surprise, Miss Winter smiled, and she seemed a whole person just then, not two darting eyes behind a white mask. "He certainly is," she agreed. "A most selfish and conceited pirate. Be sure to play rough with him, won't you?"

CHAPTER SEVEN

SEEING HIMSELF succeed at giving orders made me bold to try. That evening, while Mrs. Sexton ran the warming pan under our sheets and Himself employed a feather as a plank to save his pirate from drowning in the washbowl, I carried a chair over to the shrouded mirror to lift the pillowcase away. As I reached for it, I saw a movement in the glass beneath the cloth: my own movement to uncover it, no doubt. But it startled me, and I decided to try my luck at assigning the task to another.

"Mrs. Sexton," I said as she gathered her things and prepared to leave for the night. "I don't believe you've noticed, but a cloth is blocking the mirror."

"Aye, it is," she grunted. And before I could say another word, she had gone and locked the door. That ended my attempt at a lady's graces, and the mirror stayed as it was.

Himself dropped off like a lamb with Rogue tucked in the crook of his arm, and how that injured figure had managed to survive the day was more than I could account for. But I had asked Mrs. Sexton to leave us a candle, and I used its light to sew by, sitting up in bed and working on Alma Augusta's pretty dress until I had it complete.

A humming caught my notice, as of an insect that had been but half crushed, so that life still stirred. I sought the offending creature to end both life and noise, but I could find nothing; it seemed to move about the room and got the better of me. I concluded that the candlelight had awakened it to a false day, but that night would restore its rest, so I blew out the candle and climbed into bed.

Two white eyes stabbed the darkness in the corner by the clothes press. I lay in terror and watched as they prowled the little chamber, and where they moved, the humming went with them. At the same time, an odor suffused the room, as of putrid, maggot-riddled flesh.

I squeezed my eyes shut and lay as still as a statue then, but the aura of evil that traveled wherever the specter moved assaulted my senses like a visible form. The darkness that hid under the skin of my dead maid appeared here naked and virulent, like a tumor grown so fat that it had corrupted the healthy tissue and consumed the entire body.

The hum drew near, next to my pillow, and the foul odor made me retch. Beside me, Himself awoke.

"Go away!" he cried. "My pirate's going to carve you up, you nasty strip of horsemeat!" The humming receded at his words, and the stench began to fade.

"Is that your ghost?" I whispered, unwilling still to open my eyes.

"The dead master with the eyes like windows," he confirmed, stretching. "Much good it does him to curse me—he hasn't hands to throttle me with."

"I like my ghost better," I said, shivering, and it was a long time before I could sleep.

The next day dawned sunny, with a riot of birdsong, and Mrs. Sexton turned us out of the house with our dinner in a napkin, saying she had work to do. As we walked through the kitchen garden, Arnby came whistling around the corner of the house, carrying a bucket and brush.

"At last we've got springtime, thanks to the two of you," he announced cheerfully. "You've made this old land bloom again with your bright young faces: she's shaking off her age and bad humor. Tomorrow's May Day, she'll be young again like you, and then the luck'll come back to this house."

"What luck?" asked Himself, propping his pirate close so the little doll could hear.

Arnby set his bucket down on top of the low stone wall. "Oh, gambler's luck, I guess you'd call it, young sir. The master of Seldom House rarely loses a wager. And then there's the luck of the land, with full harvests and fine weather. We can't have that for nothing, you know." He caught my eye and laughed. "But I'd better hush my talk, or the little maidie will call me a superstitious old fool. If you're wishing to ramble, stay on the slope above the house where you see the sheep grazing. Don't go downhill or around to the other side, the path's slick with mud, and all the rain has filled the bogs to bursting."

We took his advice and climbed into the pasture, the lambs stopping their play to watch us go by and the birds flying up from the grass at our feet. There I sat and stitched Alma Augusta's petticoat, with the sun warming me and my hair blowing into my face, while Himself ran and shouted and called me at least a dozen times to help him find his pirate.

"He'll be eaten if you don't take care," I warned. "Just you wait till a sheep finds him first."

"Rogue will run the sheep through with his arrows," he countered, and I owned that the creature would probably regret the meal.

At length, Himself grew impatient with my sewing and teased me to join him in his play, and we resolved to climb the ridge to its highest point. "What shall we find there, do you think?" he asked excitedly, running races with himself while I labored up the steep slope.

"More of what we see already" was my sensible reply when I had breath to spare for it. Then the slope became easier, and then it became level ground, and the wind met us with a great rush.

On the other side of the ridge, green crests of hills tumbled away into the distance like so many moss-covered cobblestones, mottled here and there with rusty turf or patches of purple heather. Black rain clouds massed in the west, but the morning sun lit the moorland so that it glowed beneath those charcoal clouds as brightly as a jewel. Turning around to look east, we saw a hazy golden sky and the shining disk of the sun shedding its beams over a great tousled counterpane of green and brown. We could see the slate roof of Seldom House down below, but the village and the watercourse at its foot were hidden in shadow.

"At my other houses," I said, "they built fences everywhere, until the land looked like it was caught in a net. Here, I can't see a fence except for the ones by the house. The land here is still free."

The wind buffeted us so that I made Himself take my hand to keep him from rolling off the ridge. We walked back a short distance and took shelter at the base of a little white cliff to eat our dinner. The sun slanted down on us, and the wind passed roaring over our heads, a clean, wholesome sound.

Himself had chased a field mouse into a hole. "First, we'll cut off your nose, and then your ears," his pirate Rogue told it. The mouse prudently remained hidden.

"Let it alone," I said. "You shouldn't make sport of God's creatures. Nose and ears, indeed! Did they crop mice where you lived before?"

"No, they cropped people." He set a morsel of bread down on a stone by the mouse's hole and watched like a cat for it to emerge.

"What, people with no noses? With their ears

cropped? How disgusting! I can't believe you've witnessed such deformities."

He looked up at me, surprised, and I saw that he had indeed witnessed these things—witnessed, and very likely cheered. There was a savage innocence in his gaze, an indifference to the very notion of suffering. I felt my blood run cold at it. No little child should look so.

"Where do you come from?" I wondered.

He poked a grass stem down the mouse hole. "From hell."

"Don't be a fool! People don't live in hell."

"I did. Look, there's someone on my roof."

Seldom House did not lie directly below us, being on a knob of land that stood out from the slope of the ridge. From our vantage, the distant roof appeared to be a tilted square, forested with pale chimney pipes and broken into many smaller surfaces that rose to ridgelines and met one another at valleys as they accommodated the gables and dormer windows. Against the dark gray roof slates, the tiny figure of a man in a white shirt stood out clearly. As we watched, the figure shortened by degrees and disappeared.

"Who was he?" asked Himself, shading his eyes

with his hand. "He has to come back, doesn't he? He can't climb down a chimney."

"Let's take a better look," I suggested.

We hurried down the slope, an activity as challenging as its ascent. The closer we came, the more difficulty I had interpreting the pitches and angles of the roof. Surely its center should not be a valley. Surely it should be the highest peak of all. And yet ridgelines and gables rose up before it, and it sank further from view.

An outcrop of rock afforded us the most advantageous prospect. Himself clambered onto it, and I crept out after him as far as I thought wise. The house was only a few hundred feet below us now, and I could make out faint lines that marked the edges of the slates.

"I think there's a courtyard beyond this side of the house," I said. "It's hard to be sure, but I think I can just make out a hint of it there; that part's tiled like the roof, but you can see it's actually the top of a wall. A little courtyard. It must lie at the back of the topiary garden. I suppose it's there to bring light into the house, but I can't recall a single window that opens onto it."

"He got off the roof, then," said Himself,

disappointed. "I wanted to catch him crawling down a drainpipe."

I made my charge come off the exposed rock before a gust of wind could knock him from his perch, and then we scrambled around its base. A familiar figure waited for us there.

Sunlight did nothing for the dead maid but reveal the worm holes in her dress. It could not drive out the darkness that filled her empty sockets—the darkness that seemed to fill her. But now I knew her name and her relationship to me. Perverted as she was from her true form, yet perhaps she had a claim to compassion.

"Who's the pretty jenny?" asked Himself, and such was my state of mind that I did not think his comment strange.

"Walk on," I told him with as much of calm as I could muster. "I'll follow directly."

He trotted along, and I waited until he was out of hearing, struggling with myself all the while. Lead us not into temptation, but deliver us from evil. Was not this dead thing evil?

"Izzy," I whispered. The mute form swayed towards me at the sound of her name, and I stepped back, fighting revulsion. "Izzy," I said again, "why do you walk? What do you wish me to know?"

The dead maid's face never changed, but a pallid arm extended, the skin decorated with patches of fuzzy mold. The slender fingers pointed, so close I could see their yellow nails, at some unseen object behind me. Hair prickling on the back of my neck, I turned.

As still as portraits, they stood in that sunlit pasture, an abomination to all things living: dozens, quite close to me, black dresses rotted and black sockets stark, a company of dead maids. It did not matter that some looked old and others very young, some tiny and others fat. These were differences in disguise, variety of costume, with no connection to the essence of their being. What that essence was could only be felt: a presence not human, not animal— a single mindless, ravenous presence that fed on decay. Only their gray skin, wetly gleaming, shiny as slugs, shielded me from the horror of what lay within them.

I ran. I flew down that hillside, and if I had fallen along the way, I could not have tumbled faster than I ran. When I reached Himself, I caught him up under one arm and never for an instant slowed down. I wonder now how I did it, for he was more than half my size, and yet I tell you he felt as light to me then as if I held a feather pillow.

I took heed of nothing until I reached the low wall of the kitchen garden and the entire household came rushing out to meet us. There I fell and had to be helped to my feet and all but carried indoors. The first thing I noticed upon returning to my senses was Himself limping beside me and cursing with great precision and vehemence, like a hardened old sinner.

"Wisht!" I gasped, reaching out to catch his coat and shake him.

"Give over," he said, dodging me. "You daft chit! I might have dropped my pirate."

Then I was in the kitchen, seated on the bench by the hearth, and four somber countenances bent over me: Mr. Ketch, Miss Winter, Mrs. Sexton, and old Arnby, who had fetched me inside.

"What happened?" demanded Miss Winter in a quavering voice. "An injury? Gash? Broken limb?"

"Not a bit of it," said Arnby. "She's seen the cold ones. You're a fool if you let her out of the house again."

CHAPTER EIGHT

I SPENT THE DAY quietly with Mrs. Sexton next to the blazing hearth, working on Alma Augusta. By afternoon, I had finished her petticoat, and Mrs. Sexton had found me a hank of sheep's wool to stitch together and shape into her hair. Himself abandoned me to visit the stables with Mr. Ketch, but he came back from time to time, sorry to lose my company, and at last brought his pincushion pirate and played at my feet.

I did not speak of the horrors I had seen. At first, I was too shocked to bring them back to mind, and then I was too worried about what they might mean. And then, I come from the servant class, where the habit of silence is strong. Telling secrets may mean starving in the street.

Himself once again demanded a real supper in the dining room, and I found the gathering every bit as awkward as the night before. Miss Winter ate daintily, so that I felt a graceless lump beside her, and acted as if she were alone in the room. Her face was perfectly composed, and one might have thought her bored, except that her eyes flitted here and there so strangely.

Mr. Ketch did not eat. He drank a good deal instead. He acted like a victim of fever, animated to the point of delirium. If he had been under my care, I should have put him to bed and sent for the doctor at once.

My charge was completely at ease. He did not appear to notice the agitation of his reluctant companions, and as for table manners, he made up his own. They disgusted us all, but I did not correct him, for fear Miss Winter should have occasion to correct me.

We had finished our simple meal, and Mr. Ketch was telling a pointless story about London when I became aware of a faint noise in the room, like the crackling fur of a cat during a thunderstorm. The odd sound moved past me, and when it drew close to Mr. Ketch, he became even more excited, until I feared he might fall into a fit.

"Why are you afraid of that little boy?" Himself interrupted.

Mr. Ketch stopped speaking and gulped down his ale. Then he poured more from a pewter jug.

"What little boy?" I asked.

"The boy standing over there." Himself gestured towards the faint noise. "I've watched him tag after Master Jack for days."

"How curious," remarked Mr. Ketch, with an attempt at a laugh. "I don't see a boy. I see a wizened horror, all teeth and hair and fingernails."

"How can a thing be all fingernails?" scoffed Miss Winter. "I see no one. I never see them," she continued in a low voice. "I feel them instead. I wonder which is harder to bear."

"He's a boy my size, with a brown face," said Himself. "He acts like he can't see me. Like the girl Tabby talked to today, the one with yellow hair. She didn't look at me either."

"You spoke with someone?" demanded Miss Winter, her strange eyes searching my face.

"I spoke with Izzy, miss. And maybe with

some—some others; I'm not sure. But I don't see her yellow hair—not as such, I mean. What I see has been dead for a long time."

"She's pretty," Himself protested.

"She was," remarked Miss Winter. "I suppose I should be grateful I don't see them."

"Why is the brown-faced boy here?" Himself asked.

"Why is any of them here?" murmured Miss Winter.

Mr. Ketch drew a deep breath. "If you must know, that boy was fond of me."

"Fond of you!"

There, I knew I shouldn't have said it. The words had slipped out before I thought. But it seemed wholly improbable that first Izzy and now a little boy should haunt this dreadful house out of love.

Mr. Ketch glared at me through bloodshot eyes and drank off his ale. "You doubt me," he snarled. "You doubt my word. You do."

"Never mind, Jackie," warned Miss Winter.

I said nothing.

"No, Flora, we see here Christianity at work, and I intend to speak about it." Mr. Ketch leaned towards her, pronouncing his *s*'s with great care. "My heathen git isn't frightened by our ghosts, but this pious little scrap of yours sees them as awful things that send her running home in terror. What are we to make of this, eh?" He favored me with a scowl. "That your churchgoing has spoiled natural innocence."

I might have asked why he saw teeth and finger-nails in his specter, but I knew not to argue with my betters.

"So you see, boy," he went on to Himself, "you're missing nothing with religion. Let them keep their guilt and their hell."

Himself was listening with interest. "I've been to hell," he said. Mr. Ketch laughed at that and poured another glass, and I felt it my duty to speak.

"Hell is a fact, and so is guilt, when a person misbehaves," I said. "It's shame enough to keep this boy in ignorance. He shouldn't be lied to as well."

"What is the truth, pray? That he should waste his life in humble servitude to others, hoping that a benevolent divinity will reward him? You won't do it, will you, my boy—you'll live just as you please." And he nodded his approval at Himself's enthusi-astic reply.

"You'll make a heartless villain of him, sir," I protested, "with no conscience to teach him kind-ness. What should happen if you stood between him and what he wanted? Should you counsel him to murder you in your bed?"

"In an instant!" thundered Mr. Ketch, slamming his fist down on the table. "I want no cowards in this house, no, by hell I don't. And you would murder me, wouldn't you, young rogue? I'm sure of it, you rascal. I tell you, there's comfort in that."

"That's quite enough, Jackie," said Miss Winter, rising from the table. "They can't tell when you tease."

The conversation raised Mr. Ketch to his old place in my charge's affections. Himself was fairly overcome with hero-worship. He was still chattering away about it as I undressed him for bed that night.

"How brave he is!" he said while I scrubbed his neck with a cloth. "Doesn't mind if I murder him. Glad of it, in fact! I hope I may do murder yet, he'll be let down if I don't."

"Start tonight," suggested Mrs. Sexton, to my complete surprise. "Tomorrow's May Day already. Bah!" she grunted as she untied the bed curtains. "I've lived too long to wait on the masters and their maids."

"Whatever can you mean?" I demanded, but she picked up the warming pan and left without tucking us into bed.

"Rogue wants to do murder," announced Himself, wriggling away from my wet cloth. "Rogue says he'll murder anyone who washes him."

"Rogue can stay nasty and full of pins if he likes," I retorted, "but I'll have no dirty feet in this bed. Come back here if you don't want to sleep on the floor."

Izzy did not haunt me that night, but other thoughts haunted me instead. I am no quick study; my thoughts take their time. As I lay in the dark, I remembered again the man in the white shirt, and the presence of the unseen courtyard.

As I lay there, I swear I could feel the house settle into its proper place around me. Nearly a week's exploration had taught me its stairways and passages, and I traveled them now in my mind. They had made no sense then; they had twisted upon themselves without meaning until I had learned their secret. Now I saw plainly that the house was not a whole entity, but rather three long, narrow buildings joined at their corners and shaped around an empty core. The barn made up the fourth side of the puzzle box. Seldom House was hollow.

As soon as I grasped this, I felt the narrow shaft at the center of the house begin to pull on my spirit like a whirlpool. It did not exist as an afterthought.

The house existed to surround it. I could feel that empty well tugging at me through the walls that shielded me from it, the black heart of this evil place, the focus of dread and mystery. I fell asleep aware of its presence, and I awoke determined to find it and learn the truth about the deadly place at last.

CHAPTER NINE

THE DAY dawned cool, damp, and windy, with low clouds bucketing across the sky. Mrs. Sexton stood at the kitchen window to watch them after she gave us our breakfast. She had prepared sweet cakes for us with warm butter and berry preserves. Himself had been so delighted that he had made his pirate kiss her wrinkled cheek.

I had left Alma Augusta in the bedroom. She looked beautiful now in her red chintz, with her fair hair coiled up in a bun; before breakfast, I had warmed her scalp over a candle and fastened on the little wig. Then I had propped her in the chair by the fire rather than bring her on my dangerous quest. Himself and his pirate saw eye to eye, but Alma Augusta and I were different. She was a lady now, and I didn't want to spoil her pretty dress.

"Let's play hide-and-seek," I told Himself. "You hide first."

I did not find him during our first several trials, for he was good at hiding and I was not seeking him. Our game gave me a pretext to roam about the house and look for the way into the courtyard. One by one, I examined the back walls of each wing, wandering the dim passages and holding up a candle to study them closely. But, try as I might, I could find no crack in the stone nor keyhole in the paneling that might indicate the presence of a door.

"I'm tired of this," said Himself after waiting patiently for me yet again. "You hide now, and I'll find you." But I proved no better at hiding than I had been at finding, and he grew disgusted with me.

Having examined the wing that held the kitchen, including the passages outside Miss Winter's rooms, I turned my attention to the wing that held the front door. The man in the white shirt had been closest to this part of the house. Perhaps he had come through a doorway to an outside flight of stairs. If so, the door must be high in the wall. I began my investigation on the top floor.

"I've stood by the banister there, watching you," announced my charge. "You weren't hiding. You meant to be rid of me. I'm master, and I shan't bear this. If you won't play properly, I'll tell Mrs. Sexton."

"All right," I admitted then, "I wasn't hiding, and I haven't been looking for you. I'll tell you what I'm doing. I'm looking for the way into the courtyard we saw, where the man in the white shirt went. I can't find a regular door, so you can help me look for cracks or keyholes, something unusual."

We had come to the room at the top of the stairs with the painted leather panels, where Himself had sulked inside the enormous buffet. It was such a lovely chamber, I thought, with its warm colors and its fine work, but my enthusiasm abated when I recalled that Izzy's ghost had appeared here. Leather panels, I mused, attempting to put her from my mind. What better material to cover a secret door?

"I see something unusual," said Himself, standing in the middle of the room. "Someone's come in here to dust."

I was running my hands over the leather, the flaking gilt from the painted flowers spangling my fingers. "Why's that unusual?" I asked.

"Because all these rooms are dusty, that's why," he said, "and this one was too. Rogue says to tell you you're thick."

Himself was right, I realized, looking around, and quite possibly so was his pirate. This chamber had been full of cobwebs and grime the last time we had seen it. Since then, the floor had been mopped, the cobwebs pulled down, and every curve of the wooden overmantel polished until it gleamed. No wonder the chamber looked so nice.

"But why?" I wondered.

"Maybe they wanted the man in the white shirt to see it looking tidy," said Himself.

"Then the door is here. Where is it? Look for cracks that make the edges of a door."

We searched for some time, but we found no cracks, and I was put to some trouble dissuading my charge from prying off the leatherwork to make his own. Finally, Himself tired of the game and sent his pirate to explore the wide fireplace.

"Don't play in the ashes," I said without turning around.

"It's clean here, too," he said from the hearth. "Do you think they scrubbed off the soot?"

"This room may not have had a fire in a hundred years. They've plenty of other rooms to heat if they wish."

"Then why did you tell me not to play in the ashes?"

Now he lay between the brass andirons so that only his calves and bare feet were visible. "It's a fearfully deep cave, Rogue," he said. "There may be monsters." After a minute, he crawled back into the room. "Rogue found a piece of moss," he said, holding it up.

The fragment looked as if it had been stepped on and then knocked off a man's boot. Perhaps it had fallen from the stones of the chimney, which was unused and might be damp. Nevertheless, moss indoors was worth investigating.

"Show me where it was," I said.

I bent below the stone lip of the mantel and discovered that the chimney was remarkably roomy. I could stand up if I wished, although I kept a hand before my face, anxious not to strike the side of a narrowing flue.

"Here's where I found the moss," said Himself, standing beside me and pointing off to the right. "And look!" He trotted into the shadow at the

right-hand side of the fireplace and kept going until he vanished from view.

"Wait!" I gasped, scrambling after him.

Ten or twelve stumbling steps in utter darkness, with cold stone walls on either side. Then came a crack of light and a gust of wind in my face. Himself had pushed open a door and was outside, with dark slates at his feet and long shreds of rain clouds scudding by just overhead.

We stood at the top of a straight flight of rusted metal steps that ran down the side of our wall, turned a corner, and continued down the adjacent wall. They were accompanied by a railing of straight iron bars higher than I could reach and so closely spaced that Himself couldn't wedge his head between the bars to see what lay below, in spite of his determined efforts to do so. Accordingly, he raced down the flight of stairs, ignoring my call, and I hastily followed.

We were in a space about twenty feet square, unroofed and defined by the four walls of the house that surrounded it. The top ten feet of the walls were covered with slates; the rest was rough brown gritstone covered with the mold, soot, and grime of centuries. Not a single window or architectural flourish

broke the monotony of the sheer walls, and their blank faces rose four stories or more around the central cavity to block the light of the overcast sky. The shadows of a mock twilight enfolded us as we descended, and I took care to watch my footing. Someone had scrubbed the steps recently, a surprising attention to pay in that neglected and dismal place.

I reached the bottom and discovered that the whole of the courtyard lay under thick moss except for a large rectangular hole and the dark earth cast up beside it. Rich, exuberant growth covered everything else with such a brilliant green hue that it appeared to glow in the dusky gloom. By the steps, the moss had been trampled flat, but most of it was pristine, a soft, delicate blanket. We were below ground level here, and the sheer walls ended in a series of arched openings that ran along the four sides like an old-style cloister. On three sides, black shadow lay beyond the arches: the cellars of the house, I assumed. In the fourth direction, I could see a glimmer of daylight in the darkness some distance away.

Himself trotted to the center of the enclosure and peered into the hole. "Stand back from there," I ordered, following him. The hole was deeper than I was tall and at least six feet on a side, with its great pile of muddy earth beside it. At the bottom was a puddle of rainwater reflecting the cloudy sky, a mirror waiting to catch a glimpse of our faces.

Two rows of rubble stretched beside the square hole, like stone fences that had tumbled down. The thick moss had swallowed them up and softened their contours. On top of the rows, small brown sticks stuck in the moss. I walked towards the nearest row, sinking into green fuzz, worrying about my shoes. Only when I saw the skull did I understand.

The brown sticks were bones. The twin rows of rubble were more bones, great ancient piles that had accumulated there for centuries. The hole was a grave, filled many times, empty now, waiting to receive a new member into this family that was related, not by birth, but by death.

CHAPTER TEN

THE GRISLY revelation left me strangely calm. I felt as if I were floating. "The dead walk because their bones are nearby," I whispered. So many bones. So many dead.

They were old, these bones, the fruit of centuries. And yet, they were so small and pitiful. Old master, old maid. Young master, young maid. The young ones had best be on their guard.

"Look at me! I'm king of the castle."

Himself had scrambled up an odd boulder that heaved its bulk out of the ground to block one of the archways. The action of water dripping down it for ages had scooped out its top so that it looked like a gentleman's chair. There sat my charge, kicking his heels and waving his pirate in the air, the young master of Seldom House, directly before the grave that had held the last young master. The grave that I was sure lay empty now to hold him. To hold the pair of us.

My composure gave way so suddenly that I thought I might scream.

"Come," I said, running to the boulder and holding up my arms to pull him down. "We need to leave before someone sees us. But we won't go up the stairs. We'll try a new way." And I pulled him towards the glimmer of daylight in the cellar.

A heavy scent of mildew assailed us there. As the light from the courtyard failed behind us, I felt my way through a forest of square brick pillars. Gravel crunched and shifted under my shoes.

"Let go, clumsy girl!" cried Himself. "You're smacking me into the poles." But I didn't dare let him go.

We came to a wall—more brick, my fingers told me—and there was an opening in it. Paving stones were under our feet then, and a good straight passageway around us. The glimmer was a beam of light now, directly ahead of us. In another minute, we came through the arched doorway I had seen in the hillside, on the path between the village and the house.

Where to run? Not to the village, surely, where the dull inhabitants would emerge from their cottages to watch our every move. Not to the ridge, where the household would doubtless spy our escape from the kitchen windows. A new direction, then, towards the barren land to the north. We might starve, but we wouldn't be murdered there. I pulled Himself off the path and hurried across the face of the hill.

"What are you about now?" he complained, dragging his feet. "I want to go back there and look at the bones. I wanted to keep a skull."

"No skulls," I told him. "What a barbaric notion! Don't tell anyone what we saw back there—it's an evil that shouldn't be talked of. We're going away this very instant. This is no fit house for Christian children."

My charge planted his feet and set all his strength against me. "Then you go. I like it here. I'm master, and that's what I want. And besides, I'm not a Christian child."

On the previous afternoon, I had run with him

tucked under an arm. Now I had the greatest difficulty shifting him. We struggled together on the hillside not fifty feet from the path, and Arnby found us there as he walked up from the village.

"What's this?" he cried, moving quickly, and soon caught up to the pair of us. I noticed that he wore a white shirt. "Little maidie," he told me, "you shouldn't be out playing in this weather. It's threatening a downpour."

"She's running away, but I'm not," said Himself. "She fair pulled my arm off. Arnby, you knock sense into her for me, you've a good broad hand."

Arnby didn't strike me, but he surveyed me darkly, shaking his head. "Always the maids," he muttered.

He marched us up the path and around to the kitchen door, where he knocked for Mrs. Sexton. "I caught them outside, running off," he told her, thrusting us into the kitchen. "A fine state of affairs that would be. You ought to take better care."

Mrs. Sexton turned back to her pots and puffed on her pipe. "Not my lookout," she grunted.

"Please don't think me ungrateful," I begged them. "I was trying to fetch help. The boy's life and mine are in danger."

"In danger, eh?" Arnby asked me. "What do you know about it?"

"I believe, sir, that Mr. Ketch and Miss Winter have brought us here to kill us."

"If you must know," said that reprobate, without turning a hair, "the old master and maid don't do the killing. They've only nominated you, in a manner of speaking. Us villagers cover you over, decently scattering the dust like folks do for any burial, but the old earth herself takes your lives to rebuild her—bone, body, and blood. Don't look so down in the mouth. You should be proud to be chosen. It's an honor to be given to the land."

I don't know how I looked. I could scarcely breathe. I gasped, "You mean to bury us alive."

"Tonight, as soon as it's full dark," he agreed. "Mrs. Sexton, take the girl and lock her in her room. I'll keep the young master with me."

The housekeeper didn't leave off her task. She blew out a cloud of smoke. "I feed 'em. I don't pen 'em," she answered.

So Arnby had to take me himself, and I saw to it that the task was not an easy one. My charge, watching me being chivvied along, set up a commotion as well. The old man was hard put, but he

wasn't rough with us—preserving our bodies un-
damaged, I suppose, for the good of the land that
would eat us.

As we battled one another down the hall, Mr.
Ketch appeared in a doorway, holding a bottle of
spirits in one hand and a glass in the other. His
face was the color of old ivory.

"What the deuce is going on?" he asked shakily.

"See that fine gentleman there, that capital fellow?" I asked Himself. "He brought you here to be
killed. He means to watch you die tonight."

Mr. Ketch went white around the mouth. "It
isn't as if I enjoy it!"

At that, the child bared his teeth and told Mr.
Ketch what he should do to him if he had the means,
employing the most picturesque and disagreeable
language I have heard from that day to this. Mr.
Ketch seemed genuinely fascinated; cheeks sagging,
eyes bulging, he drifted along behind us, unable to
tear himself away.

"Give me a hand with this pair," puffed Arnby,
hauling us up the steps, but Mr. Ketch took care
not to come within reach. "Whey runs in your veins
these days. A fine yoke you two are, you and that
harpy yonder, there's no knowing which is the man
and which is the maid! The luck'll leave this house

if you don't look sharp about it. I'm sorry I've lived to see the old ways so treated and the earth so badly used."

He pushed us into our room and locked the door. We shouted and beat our fists against it, but to no avail: we heard his boots clump back down the stairs.

I found that my teeth were chattering, and I couldn't make them stop. I climbed the wooden stepladder, undid the ties, and let the green curtains shield the bed. Then I lay down in the gloom with my knees drawn up to my chin, shivering as though I had a fever.

Himself parted the curtains and crawled into bed beside me. He looked as if he might have been crying. "I can't find Rogue," he complained. "It's your fault I lost him, you dragged me about so."

I might have observed that Arnby had done plenty of dragging, but instead I took him into my arms. He was shivering too.

"I'm sorry," I whispered, and I meant it.

"Sing me a song," he said as we lay there together in the darkness.

"Bless you! I can't sing," I said, half sobbing.

"I knew a beautiful lady," he whispered to me. "Her hair was soft, and she used to let me stroke it.

I loved to hear her sing; I used to tell her to, and she sang just to please me."

"Was she your mother?" I asked, but he didn't answer.

"Then it was all shouts and screams and fire everywhere, just like they say hell is, and devils running into the houses and killing people. I hid in the bread oven, and they didn't find me there. I heard her call me, and then I heard her scream, so I crept out to see. She was on fire, waving her arms in the air, and two devils took their spears and pushed her into the hottest flames, making a joke of her burning. I ran and hid, and ran and hid some more, and I left the beautiful lady behind in hell."

I meant to tell him that this was not hell, although it sounded horrible. But before I could, he spoke again.

"Are we going to die tonight, truly?"

I didn't answer, but only wept.

"Well, I'm not sorry," said Himself. "I like it here, and I'll be master at any rate; dead or alive, I'll stay with the house and the land. I can join the other ghosts and play tricks on the living. I'll soon have Master Jack's hair turning white."

That made me laugh through my tears.

The little boy twined his arms around my neck

and snuggled close to me. "We'll lie just like this when they cover us up, won't we?" he whispered. "And then we won't be scared. And I've a score to settle with that old master who had the fit. I hope when I'm dead my hands will stop slipping through him."

I felt sorrier for the poor child at that moment than I had ever felt before, and my pity for him dried my tears. The thought of dying terrified me, but I knew the promises, and I had faith that God's mercy would see me safe to the kingdom of heaven. My bones would be here, but I would be with the justified who sang before the throne of the Lamb.

But this poor heathen boy knew nothing of that. He had no greater prize to hope for beyond this world than the privilege of brawling with a ghost. If I could not save my charge's body, I could still save his soul. And yet, how should I express the invitation so that it would fit into his faulty under-standing? Asking him to renounce his evil ways wouldn't do. We had no time for proper instruction.

I sat up and pushed aside the curtain. A gleam of golden light came through. I climbed down the ladder, took up Alma Augusta from the chair next to the hearth, and laid her gently in the hiding place beneath the clothes press. Beside her, I placed

Izzy's humble knitted sock. I owed the dead that much. And all the while, I pondered what to say.

Himself sat on the edge of the bed now, holding back the curtain, watching me with those lively black eyes. My heart softened again at the sight of him. After all, he was a good boy.

I walked to the washstand and hefted the pitcher. "This land isn't so much," I said. "Shouldn't you like to inherit a kingdom?"

It was all a matter of asking the right question.

CHAPTER ELEVEN

Arnby came for Himself when dusk fell, at the head of a group of village men. But I held my charge fast and wouldn't let them take him.

"You're throttling me, you ninny," he complained.

"The boy's too young. I won't leave him," I said. "He needs me by his side."

"That's a good lass," said Arnby. "You'll be by his side, never fear. He just comes in a different way, is all."

"If you don't turn me loose," said Himself, "I'll

kick you in the shins." So I released him and let the men take him away.

Next, a group of women came, led by the one who had touched me with her thimble, and they brought me to the room with the fine leather paneling. Miss Winter was already there.

Justice compels me to give Miss Winter her due: she looked particularly handsome that evening. She had taken pains with her hair, and she wore her black dress with a poise that none of the clay-faced village women could emulate. She came to stand beside me, but she did not look at me. None of them looked at me.

A hand waved from the fireplace, and the company grew still. The woman who had fetched me from my room beckoned to Miss Winter, who bent gracefully beneath the mantel and disappeared into the hidden corridor. Then the woman beckoned to me. I ought to have bolted and made them chase me down, but such a course of action did not occur to me. I could scarcely stand on my feet as it was; I could not have run just then even to save my life.

I walked down the narrow tunnel, following the light of Miss Winter's lamp, and stepped outside behind her. A passing wind whipped at my skirt, and the night sky arched above me, with a bright moon and pinpricks of stars shining through patches of shimmering cloud. I suppose I must have stopped just then to gaze at them because a grim-faced woman with a guttering torch prodded me to keep walking.

The rest of the women and girls filed out behind me, and we made our way down the steps. Meanwhile, the men and boys were emerging from the archways below, presumably having come through the underground passage.

Miss Winter picked her way delicately along the edge of the open grave next to one of the piles of bones, and the lead woman signified, with grimaces and gestures, that I should take my place by her side. I felt dizzy so close to the yawning pit; it seemed that I walked above a precipice. Himself and Mr. Ketch were taking their places opposite ours, the latter but a hollow-eyed remnant of the bright, good-looking gentleman who had charmed me upon his arrival. The villagers packed together into a tight crowd one or two paces back from us, and Arnby walked to the mound of dirt, holding a spade.

I saw my young charge looking at the grave, and fierce, hot tears scalded my eyes. He was only a little boy, a very little, half-famished boy, with scrawny limbs and thin hands no stronger than a bird's wing. Did no one in this company understand the meaning of compassion? Was no one here capable of pity? I left my place and walked briskly to the head of the grave. "Come here, boy," I ordered. And Himself came to me with relief shining in his eyes, although he resisted when I would have embraced him.

"Here now," said Mr. Ketch uncertainly, drifting towards us. He reeked of spirits, and his footing was unsteady.

"Doesn't matter," rumbled Arnby, and he pushed by to stand between us and Mr. Ketch, perhaps to avert a drunken tumble into the grave should Mr. Ketch attempt any further movement.

"The Master of Seldom House," Arnby intoned, "having enjoyed the luck of the land and lived by our honest labor, is called upon to fulfill the contract he made when he took his place in the Master's Seat. Master, do you and your maid stand ready to perform your office?"

"Oh, aye," quavered Mr. Ketch in a thick accent quite unlike his accustomed gentlemanly tones. Miss Winter favored him with a withering look of contempt.

"But you have brought others," continued Arnby, "who have accepted their positions and taken their place as your proxies in this house."

Little choice we had in the matter, I said to myself as I squeezed my charge's hand reassuringly.

Mr. Ketch nodded gravely several times and then, realizing he had to speak, trebled, "Yes." Miss Winter rewarded him with another venomous glance.

"And do you guarantee that the proxy who takes your place as master is at liberty to dedicate his allegiance to these rites, free from the bonds of Christian service?"

"Oh, yes," said Mr. Ketch, brightening. "No trouble over that one. Ain't that right, my little heathen git?"

"He's no heathen," I declared, "and fie on you for making light of it! You would have sent him to his death unsanctified. I christened him this very day. His hair is damp yet."

Every face turned towards me, with an awestruck expression, as though I had spoken with the tongues of men and of angels. The entire gathering stared with open mouths, while the moment stretched on and on.

Then Mr. Ketch gave a high-pitched giggle.

"She's lying," he said, quick and breathless. "She didn't! She can't do that."

Beside me, Arnby set down the spade.

"Do you think so? I don't," he replied, the picture of calm. "This good, honest girl wouldn't tell an untruth. And as to doing, of course she can. Every man his own priest, eh, little maidie?" To my surprise, he gave me a wink.

"But she didn't, she didn't," said Mr. Ketch rapidly. "He wouldn't have it, I tell you." He lurched forward and threw himself on his knees before the little boy, so that the two of them were eye to eye. "Tell them you didn't let her pour water on you," he begged. "I know you wouldn't have it."

Himself looked at him and then up at me, puzzled. "But she promised me a kingdom," he said.

Mr. Ketch shrank back, his mouth wobbling. Arnby spoke quickly in the silence.

"So that's how it's to be. John Cookson, you had fair play, but she's a canny lass, and it's on your own head for squandering the luck. You made the promise, and you ratified the contract. Time to show a good spirit."

"But . . . but . . ." sputtered Mr. Ketch, "but I've been christened, too!"

"Have you? Have you, now?" Arnby laughed.

"Then shame on you for a weakling! Your parents suffered in prison for the privilege of not baptizing you."

"Not then," babbled Mr. Ketch. "Not then; in London. And your spies there never knew." He attempted, I think, a triumphant smile, but what emerged was half a grin and half a titter. "So you see where you are," he said, turning to the crowd. "You've got no master at all."

At last, my charge found something in the conversation to understand. "*I'm* master," he said resolutely.

"You've been disqualified, my boy," Arnby informed him. "You're christened, so you forfeited your chance."

Himself turned to glare furiously at me and gave me a painful pinch. I smacked his hands for it, and Arnby caught us by the shoulders and gave us both a warning shake. "As for you," he said over our heads to Mr. Ketch, "you're wasting our time. You know as well as I do that once you've sat in the Master's Seat yonder, you might become Archbishop of Canterbury if you like, but it makes no difference to us."

The Master's Seat. Arnby had nodded at the curious boulder Himself had climbed to be king of the castle. Himself had sat in the Master's Seat already, and before his christening, too. He wasn't disqualified after all.

To my horror, I saw my charge gazing on the boulder and reaching the same conclusion. He turned to Arnby. He meant to speak and kill us both. I bent to distract him, but he was too smart for me, and he shrugged out of my grasp.

What would have happened next makes me shiver yet to think of, but just then, Miss Winter began to laugh.

She had stretched out her hand to point at the terrified Mr. Ketch, and her whole body convulsed to do it: a loud, ghastly, raucous sound, half a scream, half the bray of a donkey. It stunned my charge as no ghost or goblin had; he flinched and put his hands over his ears. Before he could think to interfere again, I threw my arms around him.

"That's enough," said Arnby, and he gestured to the men standing nearby. They stepped forward with coils of rope.

Miss Winter did not seem to feel the loops of cord; she had eyes only for her partner's pitiful terror. On and on went her laughter, while the men bound her hands and feet, until the slate tiles rang with it. Her mouth stretched wide, and the screeching rose higher and higher, until it ceased to be a human sound. Then three strong fellows picked her up and slung her into the grave, and the laugh stopped with a splash and a thud. I drew breath again and found I had tears on my cheeks, and I prayed God the fall had broken her neck.

Mr. Ketch was stammering nonsense now, shreds of phrases meant to be arguments no doubt, but strung together so that they were robbed of meaning. The men threw him into the pit next, and the jabber went on in the darkness below. "Look lively," commanded Arnby, handing the spade to the person nearest and gesturing towards the pile of earth. The fellow dug out a great clump and cast it into the pit, and the jabber broke up into coughing.

One by one, villagers took turns with the shovel, ignoring the groans and mindless babble, the splashing and slithering. Gray-haired matrons and slender girls took up the spade. Boys dropped dirt in by cupped handfuls. Slowly and methodically, they went about the work of filling in the hole in which their fellow creatures lay. I cannot describe the horror of their indifference.

Afraid of losing my reason, I stopped my ears and shut my eyes. The single thought consuming my energies was a frantic resolve to quit this place, a resolve so powerful that my muscles tightened and my legs shook with the desire to run. Himself would assert his right as master, claiming he had been on the Master's Seat before he was christened, but he was young, and my word would count against his. I would lie—I would have to lie—there was no help for it. And then we would be free.

The odd boulder named the Master's Seat took hold of my imagination then. I glanced towards it, and it seemed to move ominously in the torchlight. Then I noticed a pale object lying across one stone armrest, and I swayed on my feet while the torches and villagers melted together into a bright red haze.

The pale object was Rogue. Himself had left his pirate behind when I had pulled him down that morning. The boy could prove he had sat on the heathen rock before he was christened. He could prove his claim as master.

I felt a terror so intense that I thought I would die of it, and yet my mind was clear. In that instant, I held as certain things I had not even guessed before. The dead maids were no friends to me. They had not come to warn me of danger. They had gathered before the sacrifice to gloat over me, the newest member of their sisterhood of death. I was the old maid now, trapped and shackled just as Miss Winter had been. I would idle out my meaningless years, choosing others to die in my place, until my bones took their turn at the bottom of the pit.

I must escape. We must escape together, the boy and I. But Arnby stood by us with a hand upon my shoulder, and the crowd pressed in all around.

Then a roar burst from the pit, and grimy hands clutched the edge of the shovel. Mr. Ketch had heaved himself upright. His face wore a slimy mask of dark mud, and his bloodshot eyes bulged from their sockets. He glared at us without the least flicker of intelligence: he was stark staring mad.

The old woman holding the spade struck out instinctively and gave Mr. Ketch a blow to the head. Arnby moved quickly to take the tool from her.

"No blood!" he commanded. "We'll have to stake him down. You and you, fetch rope and stakes. You two, jump in with him. Wrestle him down, no fisti-cuffs now, the blood needs to stay in the body."

As soon as Arnby moved from my side, I said in my charge's ear, "Let's play hide-and-seek to vex the old man and pay him back for locking us up."

I pulled the boy through the ring of villagers, who had no thought to spare for us in the excitement of Mr. Ketch's resurrection. We hurried around the back of the crowd, heading for the stairs. But once there, I dragged Himself to a stop.

"What ails you?" he whispered.

"Can you not see them?" I asked.

The dead maids crowded the stairs from top to bottom. Their gray faces were blank, and their motionless forms bespoke no eagerness by natural means, yet a powerful feeling rolled through me from them, a single horrid sensation of greed. One spirit ruled all their shapes; their own spirits were gone. Only the shadow remained in possession of their empty husks.

"Over here," I said to Himself and, holding hands, we darted through the nearest archway into the open cellars beneath the house. The many torches of the villagers standing by the pit illuminated the gravelly space, and each squat square pillar cast a dozen shifting shadows, until the ground fairly seethed with flickering forms.

I hurried towards the tunnel we had passed through that afternoon, but now it was Himself's turn to stop. "So many!" he whispered in consternation.

I saw no figures in the dark opening before us,

but I could feel the presence of the dead masters. I could feel their passion and violence, the evil and gloomy despair, and the mindless force living through them that yearned for the sacrifice as a starving man yearns for food. Necessity made me brutal, however. We must get through. "You wanted to take them on," I reminded the little boy. "Don't be a coward now."

He bared his small teeth, but then gave a shudder. "Not all at once," he groaned.

I was frantic with fear, and for an instant I thought of leaving him behind. But I couldn't do that to the motherless child. I knelt before him and drew him close.

"I'll help you," I promised. "Wrap your arms tight around me. Then it'll be just as you said—we won't be scared, and we'll take on these ghouls together."

He nodded and threw his arms around my neck.

Half carrying, half dragging him, I stumbled into the passageway crowded with black-hearted spirits. Fiery eyes seemed to glitter in the gloom, and puffs of wind whispered and plucked at me from all directions, tugging at Himself as though they would have me drop him. The air grew thick with a foul stench,

until I thought I should suffocate, and sparks show-
ered behind my eyelids from the effort of carrying on.
But I held fast to my charge and drew courage from
his trust in me. They should not have him while I
could prevent them.

Then a breeze flowed over us, cool and sweet.
We were outside, on the path to the village, and the
moonlit night stretched high over our heads and
touched the distant hills. I set my charge on his
feet, and we ran down the path together. We raced
through the silent village and reached the boats
pulled up on the shingle, with the water purling
quietly a few feet away.

I unhooked the canvas cover from Arnby's boat
and pushed it back. "Hide," I said to Himself. "Arnby
will never think to look for us here. He'll be so angry
to know that we chose his own boat."

Himself dove under the canvas, and I set my
weight against the bow, but my size was against
me. The boat didn't stir.

Now I heard footsteps crunching on the shingle.
I huddled against the boat and screwed my eyes
shut, praying for this one kindness, that the steps
would pass me by. But they came up to the boat
and stopped. Only the sounds of night and water
remained. After a long moment of waiting, I could

endure no more. I peeked through my hands to see who it was.

Mrs. Sexton stood gazing down at me, her pipe between her teeth. She had no need to ask what I was doing.

I got to my feet, miserable, crushed with disappointment, spreading my hands in a hopeless gesture. "I can't launch the boat," I said.

For a few seconds, she considered me. Then she bent, set her shoulder to the bow, and pushed with such force that the gravel screeched beneath the hull. She scooped me up and flung me, and I landed in loose canvas folds. The boat swayed and rocked with my weight.

I sat up. The bank was slipping by with alarming speed. Mrs. Sexton was already lost in the darkness. Only I thought I saw, as I gazed astern, a curling wisp of pipe smoke shimmering in the moonlight as it mounted up to the star-filled heavens.

Himself's head popped up, and he rapidly unhooked the rest of the canvas and stowed it in the bottom of the boat. "Don't sit at your ease," he ordered. "Take an oar! We'll pull for the bank yonder."

I took both oars from him. "We'll stay here where the water is swiftest."

"You're a fool, and you shouldn't have brought

us here," he said angrily. "We can't row against this current. I want to go home. I want to sleep in Master Jack's bed tonight and laugh at him when he haunts me."

"What a ghastly notion!" I exclaimed. "An idea unbecoming in a Christian. We shan't go back to that place, tonight or any night. We're free of it forever."

"Free! I don't want to be free of it, and it shan't be free of me. I own it now that Master Jack is in the ground. I inherited it, just as you said."

"A grave and two piles of bones, and ghouls and demons by the dozen," I said. "That's a fine inheritance!"

"My house and my land, and my luck," he retorted. "And you are my maid—you have to do as I bid you. Pull for the bank, or we'll lose the way. Streams like ours are flowing together, and we'll have trouble following the proper one back."

He peered worriedly at the dark water, measuring the distance to the shore. His anxiety gave me comfort: boats he might know, but he plainly could not swim.

"I quit your employment," I said. "I'm not your maid anymore. The honor is scarcely worth the promise of a living grave at the end. But never fear,

I mean to be a good friend to you, and that's why we're not going back."

"Then who wants you for a friend?" howled the little wretch. "What good is a friend who won't follow orders? Run away, then, you coward, if that's what you want, but leave me on the bank yonder."

I could perhaps have done it and kept the boat afloat, but I remembered that masters and maids came in a set. If Himself went back to be master, they might hunt me down. Besides, he was too young to understand what was best for him.

"Never mind that," I said. "We'll find a properly run house, and we'll live happier there than at Seldom House, though we might be bootblacks. And we'll see you instructed, too, and lose your heathen ways. You'll see—you'll thank me in time."

"Thank you? I'll curse you every day, you damned lying slut!" he cried. "I don't want to be a bootblack! And you may take your heaven back and keep it for yourself, and I hope you rot in hell with it! I don't want heaven! I want to go home!"

He burst into furious tears then, and went on blaspheming like a lost soul. I tried to soothe him, but he was inconsolable at his imagined loss. At length, the unnatural whelp sobbed himself to sleep.

That night was an experience for which I scarcely

have words, so far removed was it from the rest of my existence. After our harrowing escape, I had no fear to spare for the stream's perils, and I listened with the greatest contentment to the quiet slap of water on rocks, the running whisper of the current, and the taps and creaks and croaks that rose with the mist around me. Overhead swung the glittering stars, and the bright moon shone down and lit the curling ripples on the water. At no time in my life have I been in greater danger from the elements, and yet if I learned that heaven is such as that night was, I should deem it a joy worth the dying.

Morning broke, clear and chilly, over a broad river, down the center of which our frail craft rode. Dawn dyed the surface of the water rose-red, and then the rising sun turned it into a burnished mirror, while fingers of mist shone like spun gold. Himself awoke and gazed morosely over the expanse of flat water. He did not return my greeting.

"Look there, a steeple in the distance," I told him. "We're coming to a town, and then we'll have a bite to eat; that'll cheer you up."

The little fellow did stand in need of cheering; it was strange to see him sitting so still. "I miss Rogue," he muttered, wiping his eyes.

"You left your pirate on that pagan rock of

theirs, that Master's Seat," I said. "I saw him last night, but I couldn't fetch him down."

Himself turned to me. "Then Arnby knows," he said. "He knows I sat in his seat and I'm master after all."

"He'll reach that conclusion, I suppose," I said reluctantly.

"Then he'll not name a new master," he said, growing animated. "He'll search for me. He'll wait till I come home."

"Home—that dismal hole?" I exclaimed. "You'll not go there again."

"And you'll not tell me what to do," he rejoined. "Masters don't take orders from maids."

"I only meant that it isn't a suitable home for you," I explained. "And Arnby is no friend to you, master or not. He locked you up, and he would have killed you last night. He doesn't want what's best for you."

"He wants what's best for my land, and so do I," he said. "I'll grow bigger and stronger, and then I'll find my way home. But you needn't worry for your precious skin. I won't take you with me. I'll find a girl who's fit to be maid."

"You're all kindness," I retorted, stung at his ingratitude. "What a fortunate young lady she'll be."

"She must sing," he declared. "And she must look better than *you*. I'll not share my grave with a slattern."

"You wicked imp!" I cried. "This is the reward for my charity! Yesterday you begged me not to leave you."

"Yesterday I didn't know you were false," he said with such a miserable expression that it touched my heart, no matter how foolish I thought him. "You tricked me with your hide-and-seek game. But you didn't mean to help me, you meant to help yourself. You knew what *I* wanted."

We reached the town, the name of which I took care not to learn. A boat hauling coal lay at anchor there, preparing to cast off, and the boatmen, seeing us adrift, snared our craft with hooks and brought us on board. When I learned they were headed downstream, we did not go ashore; instead, I offered to knit stockings for every man of the crew in exchange for our food and passage.

Thus we came safe out of that accursed country, with not a footprint left behind to tell of our passing, nor a scent for the bloodhound to catch.

CHAPTER TWELVE

THAT IS ALMOST all I have to tell. My travels over
the succeeding months brought me to Haworth,
where I found my surname among the new graves
and Susanna Aykroyd welcomed me as family. Indeed, she had need of family then, with her parents
carried off by infectious fever scant weeks before,
and her brother George gone away to be a soldier. I
taught her to knit as I did: Ma Hutton's style of
knitting was unknown in these parts, and our
stockings fetched a good price. She taught me to
read and write in return, and we soon opened our

own knitting school, with her running the business side, as she was older, and me teaching the children.

We gave out that we were sisters to lend an air of stability to our establishment, a harmless fiction that has long ago been accepted as truth, for Haworth is a modern town, all bustle and go; none can be acquainted with every one of its thousands of inhabitants, and the gossips have more than they can do to keep track of the bastard babies born in our midst before death can snatch their latest news away. And then, Susanna and I have been good sisters over the years, truer and more amiable relations than many bound by blood. As our school was a modest success and our needs were few, it follows that we prospered.

For almost ten years, I did not tell a living soul of the events at Seldom House; nor did I think of them if I could avoid it. As the seasons came and went, I stopped scanning the streets for Arnby's round face, and I began to believe that the sordid details of this narrative were episodes sealed in the past. But one fine summer evening not long after a shower of rain, I saw a woman standing in the street outside our rooms, looking up and down, as if she were unsure of the address. While the woman thus wavered irresolute upon the cobblestones, a man tramped by carrying a lantern, and I saw her features plainly. It was Miss Winter.

Death had not been kind to that proud creature. Her dress was filthy, and webs and dirt clung in her hair. The glittering eyes that had told of her fear were gone, replaced by smooth pools of shadow. An instant she stood so, caught in the light of the lantern. Then she melted into the stones of the street. But I felt her spirit near me still, the spirit of the land itself. After nearly a decade of peace, I felt blind hunger flow through me from the dark places of the earth, and I knew that another sacrifice was taking place at Seldom House.

My reason all but fled in the days that followed: brain fever, the doctors called it. Susanna was forced to close down the school for the time being and devote herself to my care. But we survived and even flourished by the change, for Amos Wood, the doctor's assistant, spoke to Susanna, and they were wed as soon as my convalescence would allow. They set up housekeeping in a little cottage not far from our old rooms and invited me to join them.

The three of us shared a happy home there for many years. The ghosts did not trouble me whilst we lived together, although they drew near at the time of the sacrifices. I would feel their presence beyond the window curtains; at such times, I took care to stay indoors. But Amos Wood had a bad chest, and he died by the seaside in 1823, whence the doctors had sent him to recover; and not long afterwards, Susanna went to Bingley to nurse her cousin Rose. In this way, I was left alone.

On an evening during the winter of 1824, I was sitting by the fireside, sighing for happier times, when I heard a faint sound at the window. I took no notice at first, for the night was tumultuous, and the window glass rattled throughout the cottage, but the sound moved from pane to pane, low yet insistent, a tapping or scratching noise. Convinced at last that it was not the action of branches in the wind, I arose, opened a little window, and leaned out to see.

An eyeless woman stood without, a most horrible visitant—the more ghastly, as she had at one time in life been excessively pretty; but the grave makes slatterns of us all. Her hair hung in untidy curls, and her slender frame stooped with fatigue, as though she traveled a weary road with no hope yet of reaching its end. Of all the maids, she alone was not in black, but wore a loose white dress. She was groping her way along a nearby window, clutching at the sill and turning her pale face with its shadowed sockets to and fro as if to catch a sound, or a scent.

Head cocked, she paused; and then, by sound or scent, she found me, and she moved towards my window in a rush. I slammed it shut and bolted it and listened while she hammered against it so hard that I thought her fists would break the glass.

Terrified, I staggered back and huddled over the fire while that hideous wanderer circled my cottage, beating on the windows one after another as the wind moaned in dreary lamentation. Never did mortal flesh spend such a night as I did then, and how my wits survived it, I do not know. But I prayed that night as I had never prayed before, and there came to mind the kindly curate of my childhood. Ghosts cannot harm the living, he seemed to whisper in my ear, and his gentle faith sustained me in my hour of need.

The first slanting rays of sunlight drove the gray-faced horror into the earth, and I bolted from my house and made for the parsonage. There I entreated the Haworth curate to take me into his household to work in exchange for my room and board. The Reverend Patrick Brontë was then bowed down with cares, a widower struggling to provide for his young children, and if there are those who call him a hard man, well, I call them liars, for no father ever watched over a family as anxiously as he. But gossips look for evil where none exists, to mirror the evil in their own soiled hearts.

And that is how I came to live in the Haworth parsonage, in peace and contentment, for the dead maids dare not enter this quiet house where a man of God turns over the pages of his Bible. Sometimes on a stormy evening I see their spirits still as they gather beside the churchyard gate. But they cannot pass the holy ground guarded by the remains of countless Christians, and my good Susanna's family among them.

I cook the meals and keep the house for Mr. Brontë, and bake the family bread, and watch over his children, my four motherless lambs. Each morning, their father does his duty to instruct them in their faith, to which I say a hearty Amen. But when night falls, and the harsh wind scours the snow from the ground and casts it against our windows, and my little ones wrap up in shawls and creep downstairs to warm their frozen fingers by the kitchen fire, then I tell them tales that their pious father cannot know, about the red-eyed Gytrash, the slavering devil dog who waits for the wicked, and about the young girl who was murdered by her lover on the moor and who roams barefoot on the bleak hills yet. And this is as it should be, that the children should learn from us both, for bright day and dark night both work together unto good.

While the wind howls, my lambs beg me to tell them again about Seldom House, with its hidden grave and its pagan rites and its catalog of masters and maids. Young Branwell plays with his toy soldiers at being the evil pirate Rogue, and Charlotte and gentle Anne throw their arms around my neck and swear that I will never be turned out of the house to face the dead maids, but they will keep me in my old age as faithfully as I keep them now. And Emily Jane sits at my knee, gazing into the fire, and asks what became of the heathen boy who escaped with me. Did he return to claim his house and lands, as he had promised to do? Did he forsake his Christian baptism to shed blood?

Myself, I fear the worst for him, since the sacrifices have continued. Perhaps the ancient Master's Seat exerted some diabolical influence that could not be undone by the water of salvation. But the truth is that I do not know what happened to the child. We parted ways within a few weeks of our escape.

I had taken him with me, first on the boat and

then through the strings of towns as I searched for a situation, but he was no longer the happy boy I had known. He had grown sullen and bitter, like a man who has seen his hopes die at the turn of a card; he did as I bade him, but if he spoke, it was to curse. I tried to love him, and I tried to cheer him, too, and show him the error of his ways, but he persisted in blaming all his troubles on me, who had stolen him from his land and his land from him. He swore he was the master yet, with the luck that belonged to the house, and I will say this, that he was very lucky, for I thought more than once I should have to watch him hang.

We had reached Liverpool on a day so hot that we longed for the weather to break, and the clouds built into towers above us without giving a breath of sweet, cool air. My charge and I were dirty and hungry, and hot and miserable besides, with our nice black clothes worn to rags already by the hard days we had seen. I ordered him to wait for me while I sought us a bite and a sup, but when I returned, he was throwing dice with some other young rascals. I chased them away, and he swore at me again, and then I lost my patience and told him to seek his living how he liked, but I would help him no longer.

"I don't want your help," he said. "I'll do better

than you. I was winning just now, and you spoiled my game."

"You'll end up on the gallows, and I won't be there to cry," I retorted, and I went about my business.

By afternoon, the towers of clouds had turned black and oily green, and the steaming heat was soon to be drowned in a violent deluge. My conscience smote me, and I went to seek the little boy again to find him shelter from the coming storm. You may imagine my dismay when I beheld him in the grip of a hale and hearty gentleman who had evidently witnessed a crime.

"Do you know this young blackguard?" asked the man when I ran up. "He's stolen my pears, but he's only a lad; he needs a good hiding, not the magistrate and the hangman. I've tried to ask him about his parents, but I can't seem to make him understand me."

At this, my former charge leered at me, and pulled a face, and jabbered away in his savage tongue.

"Oh, sir," I said, "your kind spirit does you credit, and I do hope you'll show him mercy yet. It's a sad tale, and if it ends on the gallows, it will be sadder still. His parents are dead; his mother was killed before his eyes, and those who should have shown him Christian charity plotted to kill him as well. The poor boy has not a soul in all the world."

"There now, that's a good lass," said the gentleman, plainly touched by my distress. "You say he's an orphan, then, and ill used," and he bent down to look Himself in the face. "You're a sturdy lad, I'm thinking, even though you are on the small side, and you look as if you have your wits about you, too. Tell us, boy, what's your name?"

The little scoundrel glanced sidelong at me and bared his teeth just to spite me. "Heathen git!" he shouted. I was furious, but the gentleman stared as if he'd seen a ghost, and his hands began to tremble.

"Heathcliff?" he said in astonishment. "Why, Heathcliff's a family name. Heathcliff was the name of my own dead son."

A moment's thought revealed his error, and I opened my mouth to speak, but by then he had made up his mind.

"I'll not leave a Heathcliff to beg for his bread in the street," he declared. "You must come home with me to Wuthering Heights." And he picked up the boy as tenderly if he had been his own son and walked away into the shadow of the storm.

EPILOGUE

Tabitha Aykroyd was housekeeper to the talented Brontë family, which gave English literature two classic novels, *Wuthering Heights* and *Jane Eyre*. The Brontë sisters thought of dear "Tabby" as one of the family, and they looked after her devotedly in her old age. She is buried in the Haworth cemetery only a few dozen yards from the vault where Charlotte and Emily Brontë lie.

This beloved servant was the daily companion of three authoresses, yet almost nothing is known about her. But the family's first biographer, Elizabeth Cleghorn Gaskell, mentioned the dark, otherworldly tales that Tabby told her young charges, and Ellen Nussey, a family friend, remembered that of all the siblings, Emily Brontë loved those wild tales the best.

Much more detailed information about the Brontës and about *Wuthering Heights*, the novel that inspired this story, is available at the author's Web site, www .claredunkle.com. You may find there photographs of Yorkshire, an analysis of the mysteries and motifs of *Wuthering Heights*, an exploration of some myths surrounding the Brontë family, and a select bibliography for further study.

ACKNOWLEDGMENTS

Heartfelt thanks to Reka Simonsen for being the Platonic ideal of editorhood—practically perfect in every way.

Warmest thanks to Patrick Arrasmith for creating the wonderfully atmospheric illustrations in this book. He has caught the dark heart of this story.

My deepest gratitude to my mother, Dr. Mary Buckalew, Professor Emerita in the Department of English at the University of North Texas, for inspiring me with a love of *Wuthering Heights* before I could even read. My mother wrote her master's thesis, *Heathcliff: A Satanic Hero,* four years before my birth, and when I was a little girl, she regaled me with thrilling stories from Emily Brontë's life and masterpiece.

Sincere thanks to Dr. Ronald Hutton of Bristol University, England. His scholarly works on paganism in the British Isles allowed me to interpret some of *Wuthering Heights*'s most perplexing passages in ways I would not otherwise have dared to do.

Special thanks to Don Shelton, collector and researcher in the field of portrait miniatures, for graciously sharing his singular knowledge.

GO FISH

CLARE B. DUNKLE

What did you want to be when you grew up?
When I was five, I wanted to be a doctor. I had one of those little doctor kits with the yellow stethoscope and pink candy pills, and was forever wrapping up my stuffed animals in gauze and performing dangerous surgeries on them.

When did you realize you wanted to be a writer?
In 2001, right after finishing the manuscript to *The Hollow Kingdom*. Before that, it didn't even occur to me.

What's your first childhood memory?
I have lots of memories from when I was two—they're supposed to erase as you age, but someone forgot to rewind my brain, I guess. I remember being carried in to wake up my father, and my mother said to me, "Give your father a big hug because it's his birthday." I didn't say anything because I think I must have been too young to talk, but I remember thinking *So what?* because I didn't know what a birthday was.

As a young person, who did you look up to most?
My childhood was chaotic, lonely, and neglected. But I was blessed with fantastic teachers and librarians who saw how

badly I needed mothering and who gave me the guidance and praise I didn't know I needed.

What was your worst subject in school?
Chemistry—hands down. I have no idea why!

What was your best subject in school?
English, which makes sense.

Also, I sat behind Libba Bray in high school English class. She usually wore her red hair in a ponytail, and she pulled her hair back in this line of four or five different-colored bands. I used to marvel at how great she looked. Even back then, she had style.

How did you celebrate publishing your first book?
You know, I don't think we did. We probably popped a bottle of bubbly, and I know I mailed copies of the book out to all my nieces and nephews.

Where do you write your books?
I wrote *By These Ten Bones* in Germany, in a rat-infested garret! Well, maybe "infested" is a bit harsh, but I certainly wrote my early books in a garret, and there certainly was a rat living on the other side of the plaster wall, in our neighbor's attic. I could hear him chewing sometimes. (He probably thought he lived in an author-infested garret.)

Where do you find inspiration for your writing?
Everywhere! Nothing is off limits.

Are you a morning person or a night owl?
I'm a night owl, but nowadays I get up at six o'clock anyway. There's so much that needs to get done.

What's your idea of the best meal ever?
Anything that ends with a piece of pie. Or starts with a piece of pie. Or consists of nothing but pie! I've made my own fruit pies and lemon meringue pies since grade school.

Which do you like better: cats or dogs?
I love dogs, but I love cats more. Dogs are complete barbarians compared to cats.

What do you value most in your friends?
I value most my friends' willingness to put up with me. That's not something I think I could handle!

Where do you go for peace and quiet?
Into my own imagination, or into a book.

What makes you laugh out loud?
Stupid puns, news anchors being pretentious, pretty much everything. I don't have a very cultivated sense of humor. Whenever something funny happens in one of my books, you can be pretty sure I was giggling while I wrote it.

What's your favorite song?
Pachelbel's Canon. I think it's what heaven will sound like.

Who is your favorite fictional character?
I couldn't choose, not with all the characters I've created for my books. In my mind, they crowd around with big eyes, like dogs in a shelter: "Pick me! Pick me!" I couldn't play favorites like that.

Aside from my books, though, I have to say that Mordion Agenos, from Diana Wynne Jones's *Hexwood,* is a fantastic character and will always be a favorite of mine.

SQUARE FISH

What are you most afraid of?
Velocity! When things start to go very fast, they worry me. (Not when I'm in control, though; then it's all right. I used to drive ninety miles an hour on the German autobahn.)

What time of year do you like best?
Autumn, when the nights get long and windy and the leaves go skittering across the street. That's when the world of the imagination draws near and touches our world.

What's your favorite TV show?
Lost. Every single episode. Even the ones that didn't make sense.

If you were stranded on a desert island, who would you want for company?
A master shipbuilder! One who also knows how to make useful things out of coconut fibers.

If you could travel in time, where would you go?
Back in time to the nearest broker's office to invest in Apple, Microsoft, and Pixar. Be honest, now! Wouldn't you?

What's the best advice you have ever received about writing?
My high school English teacher, Willa Mae Burlage, taught me to picture my audience before I start to write. Since writing is communication, we have to understand where it's going if we want it to be effective.

What do you want readers to remember about your books?
I don't care if readers remember my name or the titles or plots of my books, but I want them to remember my characters

always. I want them to think of my characters as if they're alive.

What would you do if you ever stopped writing?
I have no clue! I'm not sure I could stop writing now. I might not get *published,* but I'm pretty sure I would still *write.*

What do you like best about yourself?
I can count on myself to handle pretty much any emergency I could think of and deal with it sensibly. I know; I've seen me do it!

What is your worst habit?
Squirming away from hard work, which is why I'm answering this question before I get around to figuring out what to say about the previous three.

What do you consider to be your greatest accomplishment?
Raising my two daughters and sharing with them the things I love, including reading.

I still remember how terrified I was when I found out I was pregnant. The idea of having to keep some zany, helpless, high-energy little being alive long enough for it to grow some good sense of its own left me hyperventilating. And now they're such gorgeous, remarkable young women. It's like a miracle!

Where in the world do you feel most at home?
In a library. Of course!

What do you wish you could do better?
Squeeze more hours into my days. I feel like I'm in one of those old movies where the time is sped up and people in black suits and bowler hats run everywhere.

What would your readers be most surprised to learn about you?

My daughter says you'd be surprised to learn that I didn't go to my prom or my high school graduation. (Bless her heart, she's lovely and popular—she has No Idea!) But I think you might be surprised to learn that I lived in Germany for seven years and visited fourteen different countries while I was there. It still surprises me to think that I had such an exciting opportunity, and I hope my life holds many more good surprises.

When a mysterious wood-carver arrives, Maddie is fascinated.
But then an ancient werewolf curse plunges her town into darkness.
Maddie must ask herself what she wants most.
And what will it cost her?
Find out the wood-carver's dark secret in

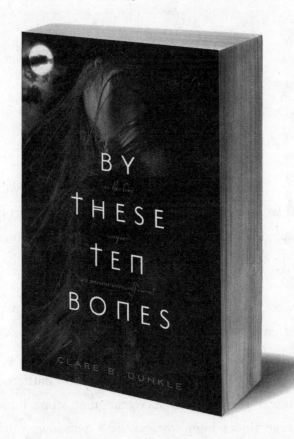

BY THESE TEN BONES

BY CLARE B. DUNKLE

1

In the far northern hills of Scotland, a gray castle stood by a narrow lake, or a loch, as it is properly called. Some castles are grand and beautiful, but this one was not. It was too small to be grand, for one thing, being the simplest type of castle. It had no moat, although its builders knew it had a natural defense: the waters of the loch at its back and swampy ground to the front. It had no palisade enclosing a fortified courtyard or lofty battlements. It was merely a large, rectangular stone building three floors high, with narrow windows through which an archer could safely shoot his foes. Carved into the rock floor of the lowest level was a primitive dungeon cell, no more than a hole, and resting above the highest level was a wooden roof that no longer kept out all the rain. A round tower clung to one corner, housing a rough spiral stair.

The wide doorway that opened into this tower lacked a door. No guards stood there, and no watch-dogs barked. A clan chief had once lived here with his family and warriors, but he had lost this valley in battle long years before. A strange old woman occu-pied his castle now, to the disgust of those few of his distant kin who still farmed the fields nearby.

A girl just old enough to be thought a young woman stood inside the tower doorway and wished that the castle still had a door to close. She was dressed in the plainest of blouses, a drab skirt that tied with a lace, and a voluminous woolen wrap that looked like a long, narrow blanket. This blanket, looped around the waist and pulled over one shoul-der, was the most important clothing of the day. Hers was checked and crossed by lines and squares of yellow, gray, and brown. If it was somewhat bet-ter made than the blankets her neighbors wore, this showed only that the local weaver had his prefer-ences. Maddie could be considered a strong favorite of his: she was his only child.

Maddie herself was not particularly striking, neither tall nor short, thin nor heavy. Her straight brown hair and brown eyes did not attract attention, and if her round face was not ugly, it also was not beautiful. At least, it was not beautiful at the moment. When she smiled or laughed, her whole appearance changed. But Maddie wasn't smiling now. She was anxious and afraid.

She had almost stepped out of the shelter of the castle tower before she saw the strangers. Four men she didn't know were walking along the gravel shore of the loch, leading two pack ponies. The first two men were small and dark, dressed as her own men dressed, wearing knee-length shirts, wrapped in blankets checked white and black, their legs bare down to their sandals. The last two men were foreigners in tunics, breeches, and boots. One of them was old, and the other was young.

Maddie shrank back into the gloom of the tower. She saw strangers very rarely. Once or twice a year, summer Travelers came through, selling or trading their craft goods. These men might be Travelers, or they might be wandering bandits, and their arrival frightened the girl. Four men were enough to do great harm in a settlement as small as hers.

The newcomers paused on the path by the grim old castle, but they didn't come toward it. The place was obviously abandoned. The path to its gaping doorway was overgrown with weeds, and the big war galley moldered on the shore nearby, its sides staved in so that it couldn't be sailed. Instead, they followed the path through boggy ground toward the low, humped houses of the settlement. Maddie could see her relatives there pointing and calling each other. A crowd began to gather. The men unstrapped their packs and started taking out their wares. They were Travelers after all. There would be new things to see, and no one would die this day.

The last stranger lingered on the stepping-stones through the bog, studying the neglected castle. Maddie stared at his odd clothing and wondered where he came from. He was tall, and his face was lean and beardless—probably, she decided with feminine disdain, because he was too young to grow a beard. He looked, however, as if he might be somewhat handsome, and he had the appeal of being completely unknown. Curious and interested, she stepped into view, but as soon as the young man saw her, he turned away.

Feeling slightly disappointed, the girl retraced

her steps. She hurried up the steep, uneven stones of the spiral stairway and darted through the tower landing into the great room beyond. "Lady Mary," she called, "Travelers are here."

In the far corner of the dusty hall, gloomy with its few slit windows, a tall, bent old woman pushed away her embroidery frame and looked up from her work. Lady Mary inhabited one small part of the place just as a hen might nest in a tumbledown barn. Throughout the three floors of the castle were cobwebs, emptiness, and whispering echoes, but here in one corner of this great room were a gentlewoman's bed and furniture.

Leaving Lady Mary to consider these unexpected tidings, Maddie hurried back down the stairs, pulling a fold of her checkered blanket loose from her waist. She draped it around herself as a shawl and brought one long edge up to veil her hair. Picking her way across the stepping-stones, she followed the path the strangers had taken through the swampy ground by the loch.

On either side of the girl rose two lines of high hills, great, green undulating walls that defined the narrow valley. Just now their steep slopes were swathed in misty tatters of cloud. Trapped between those hills, like a long silver knife blade, lay the quiet waters of the loch, with the gray castle on its gravel shore and the flat, waterlogged bog land at its head.

The settlement lay beyond this bog on slightly higher ground, its fields spreading out around it and climbing the knees of the nearest hills. A small, shallow stream ran along its edge before vanishing into the bog and filtering into the loch. A dozen low turf houses, some longer and some shorter, were scattered across the muddy ground without any apparent pattern. Sheep and chickens wandered in and out of them, seeking their daily bread, and a few shaggy cattle grazed nearby.

Just now the little community was in a state of high excitement. The townspeople thronged the open land close to the bog to see what the Travelers had brought. Hooped milking buckets and harness ropes lay on the ground, along with fine silver knives and horn spoons. The old foreigner in breeches stood over a display of wooden ware: two-handled cups, butter makers, and small chests and boxes, their surfaces carved with complex patterns. Some diminutive saints stood on the grass beside them, their wooden faces serene.

Maddie spotted the beardless stranger again. He

had unslung his own pack and laid it by his feet, but he was carving rather than selling. He sat on a boulder a little distance away from the crowd, ignoring it completely. He was fashioning a figure with a thin, curved knife, shaving off a bit here and there.

The wood-carver was grown to a man's height, and his shoulders were broad, but Maddie doubted he could be much above her own age. There was a fragile quality to his hands as they turned the wood. They were bone-white, the fingers long and slender. There was a fragile quality, too, to the hunch of his lanky shoulders. Shaggy black hair fell into his face as he bent over his work. Maddie watched him for a long minute, but he never looked up.

A quiet belch at her elbow recalled the girl to her surroundings, and she glanced back to find the old man watching her indifferently. His wrinkled face was none too clean, and his cloth cap was unspeakable, but it was perhaps better than the long, grimy gray hair that it hid. "You don't see what you want," he proffered in a thick accent, "tell me, and the boy can make it."

Lady Mary was by Maddie's side now. The old woman had taken a few moments to augment her attire. A fine damask overdress covered her plain linen dress now, and her white hair was tucked into a dusty black velvet coif. Elegant in a way that their chief's own family had never been elegant, and dressed in a style that the local people had never understood, she commanded immediate attention from the strangers.

"And what would my lady like to see?" inquired the old man, leaning forward, his faded blue eyes suddenly greedy.

"This carving work," observed the woman. "It seems quite unusual."

"It is, it is," agreed the foreigner, stooping and retrieving a little box with alacrity. "He does handsome work, the boy does, whatever your heart can wish. This here," and he ran his greasy finger over the interlacing pattern on the box top, "this is the finest style. Tapestries ain't the taste anymore, carved paneling is the thing. Last year we worked for the Archbishop of Glasgow, carving panels to his study. He begged us not to leave, says he can't find any to match the work."

The regal woman considered this unlikely tale, her eyes, like Maddie's, on the young man in question. The wood-carver didn't look up to acknowledge their interest. He kept right on carving his fig-ure as if he were the block of wood.

"But what am I to do," sighed Lady Mary, "an old woman in my rustic hermit's cell? I have no place for paneled walls."

"You have a chest that he can carve for you?" suggested the seller. "Or a box that he could work?" She nodded, her thin cheeks flushed, and the pair walked away from the crowd to make the bargain.

Maddie stood where they had left her, feeling jealous. A weaver's family was far from rich, and she couldn't even dream of owning carved chests. Then she saw something strange.

Sensing the pair's departure, or perhaps seeing their shadows move by him on the grass, the silent wood-carver glanced up quickly to study Lady Mary. His lean face was the color of bones, and his eyes were the clearest, brightest green. There was caution in those eyes—intelligence, too—and he stared after the old woman hungrily, as if he were learning her by heart. One long, penetrating glance, and he was working at his carving again as if he had never stopped.

The display of wooden ware was unattended, and the curious Maddie stepped close. "I can give you a linen kerchief for this one," she offered, pointing to a small, two-handled drinking cup. The peculiar young man didn't look at her. "Or maybe fifty," she continued, but he didn't appear to have heard.

"Can I see what you're making now?" she asked, walking over and stopping in front of him. "A tree? Why a tree? What is it for?" He didn't slow his work, the small, pale curls of wood falling onto his knees.

"Let me look at it," Maddie demanded, reaching down to take the carving from him. He didn't let it go, but he didn't look up, either. All she could see of him was black hair. "I want to buy it," she said stubbornly, trying to pull it away, but those white fingers had a firm grip on the little trunk.

"He don't ever speak, miss," warned a matter-of-fact voice, and she turned, blushing deeply, to find the disheveled old man by her side.

"Oh, I'm sorry," she exclaimed and started to step away, but those long fingers released the carving and left it in her hands. She turned it and stared at the intricate detail and lyrical expression that could make even a tiny fruit tree seem a beautiful, wonderful thing.

"You want that carving, miss?" asked the old man. He took it in his own hand and studied it dubiously. "A farthing for it, or its worth in goods." Maddie shook her head. She had no farthing or goods. A weaver's daughter couldn't come home with a useless statue. But what a canny little thing it was, to be sure. The regret showed on her face.

"Ah, now," he grunted, relenting, "tell me this. Who brews a strong drink here?"

"Little Ian makes the water of life."

"That's fine. Here's a groat. Just take this empty flask to him and have him fill it for me, and you can have the carving."

Maddie started off with a will, but curiosity overcame her. She quickly turned and looked back. The wood-carver was staring at her. She caught a swift impression of that extraordinary white face and those piercing green eyes before he dropped his head to stare at his hands. All that talent, and so sadly afflicted. What a tragedy. She walked off to find Little Ian.

The old man took advantage of a lull in the crowd's attention to turn to his prized craftsman.

"You carving trees out of trees now?" he asked perplexedly. "What's wrong with you, boy, you gone daft?"

But the strange wood-carver didn't answer a word. His attention was elsewhere. He was watching the girl make her way through the bystanders until she disappeared.

Six chilling tales

AVAILABLE FROM SQUARE FISH

The Adoration of Jenna Fox
Mary E. Pearson
ISBN: 978-0-312-59441-1
$8.99 US / $11.50 Can

What happened to Jenna Fox?
And who is she, really?

The Compound
S.A. Bodeen
ISBN: 978-0-312-57860-2
$8.99 US / $11.50 Can

Eli's father built the Compound to
keep his family safe. But are they
safe—or sorry?

Dead Connection
Charlie Price
ISBN: 978-0-312-37966-7
$7.99 US / $10.25 Can

Can Murray's ability to talk
to dead people help him find
a missing cheerleader?

Holdup
Terri Fields
ISBN: 978-0-312-56130-7
$8.99 US / $11.50 Can

The most dangerous thing at Burger
Heaven should be greasy food,
not a maniac with a gun.

The Love Curse of the Rumbaughs
Jack Gantos
ISBN: 978-0-312-38052-6
$7.99 US / $8.99 Can

Ivy has two great loves, her mother
and taxidermy.

Zombie Blondes
Brian James
ISBN: 978-0-312-57375-1
$8.99 US / $11.50 Can

All of the girls in Hannah's
new school are blonde and
popular—and dead.